Charlotte Elliot

Selections from the Poems of Charlotte Elliott

Charlotte Elliot

Selections from the Poems of Charlotte Elliott

ISBN/EAN: 9783337408718

Printed in Europe, USA, Canada, Australia, Japan

Cover: Foto ©Andreas Hilbeck / pixelio.de

More available books at **www.hansebooks.com**

SELECTIONS

FROM THE

Poems of Charlotte Elliott,

AUTHOR OF "JUST AS I AM."

WITH A MEMOIR BY HER SISTER,

E. B.

LONDON:

THE RELIGIOUS TRACT SOCIETY:

56, PATERNOSTER ROW; 65, ST. PAUL'S CHURCHYARD;
AND 164, PICCADILLY.

PREFATORY NOTE.

THE writer of this brief Sketch has been very reluctant to bring herself in any way before the public; and it is only after having been repeatedly urged, that she has, at length, consented to write these imperfect recollections of her beloved sister's life. The difficulty has been great, because those have passed away who would gladly and efficiently have assisted her, or themselves have undertaken the work. As it is, she has been obliged to rely on her own memory in reference to years long since gone by, assisted only by some scanty private memorandum, and some few of her sister's letters accidentally preserved; for a large collection—some of a highly interesting character—had been destroyed by her own hand during the last two or three years of her life, chiefly lest they might tend to any self-exaltation, so truly was she humble in her own esteem, and jealous of all that might foster vanity and pride.

These circumstances must be the writer's apology for bringing before others some very sacred memorials of a most rare affection, which she would willingly have withheld, had not others considered that they develope her beloved sister's mind more truly than any attempted description could have done.

PREFATORY NOTE.

THE writer of this brief Sketch has been very reluctant to bring herself in any way before the
public ; and it is only after having been repeatedly
urged, that she has, at length, consented to write
these imperfect recollections of her beloved sister's
life. The difficulty has been great, because those have
passed away who would gladly and efficiently have
assisted her, or themselves have undertaken the work.
As it is, she has been obliged to rely on her own
memory in reference to years long since gone by,
assisted only by some scanty private memorandum,
and some few of her sister's letters accidentally preserved ; for a large collection—some of a highly interesting character—had been destroyed by her own
hand during the last two or three years of her life,
chiefly lest they might tend to any self-exaltation, so
truly was she humble in her own esteem, and jealous
of all that might foster vanity and pride.

These circumstances must be the writer's apology for
bringing before others some very sacred memorials of
a most rare affection, which she would willingly have
withheld, had not others considered that they develope
her beloved sister's mind more truly than any attempted
description could have done.

"Just as I am."

"Him that cometh to Me I will in no wise cast out."

John vi. 37.

Just as I am—without one plea
But that Thy blood was shed for me,
And that Thou bid'st me come to Thee—
 O Lamb of God, I come!

Just as I am—and waiting not
To rid my soul of one dark blot,
To Thee, whose blood can cleanse each spot—
 O Lamb of God, I come!

Just as I am—though toss'd about,
With many a conflict, many a doubt,
Fightings and fears within, without—
 O Lamb of God, I come!

Just as I am—poor, wretched, blind;
Sight, riches, healing of the mind,
Yea, all I need, in Thee to find—
        O Lamb of God, I come!

Just as I am—Thou wilt receive,
Wilt welcome, pardon, cleanse, relieve,
Because Thy promise I believe—
        O Lamb of God, I come!

Just as I am—Thy love unknown
Has broken every barrier down;
Now to be Thine, yea, Thine alone—
        O Lamb of God, I come!

Just as I am—of that free love,
The breadth, length, depth, and height to prove,
Here, for a season, then above—
        O Lamb of God, I come!

C. E.

CONTENTS.

Contents.

Contents.

Contents.

x

Contents.

Contents.

BIOGRAPHICAL SKETCH.

CHARLOTTE ELLIOTT, the gifted writer of the well-known Hymn "Just as I am," was born 18th March, 1789, and died September 22nd, 1871. She was the third daughter of the late Charles Elliott, Esq., of Clapham and Brighton. During many years her parents formed the centre of a very interesting religious circle at both those places. Her uncle, the Rev. John Venn, was rector of Clapham; and her mother, Mrs. Elliott, was the eldest daughter of the Rev. Henry Venn, of Huddersfield and Yelling, one of the leaders of the religious awakening in the last century, and to her, as Eling Venn, are addressed many of the letters that appear in the published memoir of his life. Her two brothers, the late Rev. H. V. Elliott, of St. Mary's, Brighton, and the Rev. E. B. Elliott, author of the "Horæ Apocalypticæ," are well known by their characters and their works.

From early years she was more or less an invalid, and consequently her life was one of much seclusion, offering but few incidents and little variety. Her life was a hidden one. She always rallied during the summer months, and was able to pay visits to friends at a distance, who loved and valued her society, and appreciated the charm of her conversation and her brilliant imagination.

Amongst those whose friendship she specially enjoyed, I must mention the Cunningham family, at Harrow; our cousin, Mrs. Batten, who was a Venn; Bishop Shirley; and the Moneys, who were specially beloved. Visits to these friends always brightened the ordinary monotony of her life; and the zest with which she entered into the beauties of scenery and the charms of intellectual society, will never be forgotten by those who knew her.

Naturally she had a strong will, but this became gradually subdued, as her religious principles deepened. Her temperament was eminently poetical; and her tender sympathy in every joy or sorrow of those whom she loved is fully testified in many of her letters and poems.

She was always exceedingly fond of music, with a very fine and delicate ear; and it was only the continual interruption of ill health that prevented the successful development of this talent, as well as the kindred accomplishment of drawing, for which she showed much taste and aptitude. In younger years her voice blended sweetly with the family choir, and to the close of life her enjoyment of music was exquisite. Such tastes as these, combined with her unusual powers of conversation, her high intellectual capacity, and her zest for every interesting subject, made her companionship very delightful and highly valued.

There was a period, before my father's final removal from Clapham to Brighton, when her remarkable talents and accomplishments made her a welcome guest in circles where she met some of the most brilliant wits and writers of the day. To one of her temperament such society as this had an almost irresistible fascination. But there was an absence of religion, if not hostility to it, in many of those with whom she was thus brought into connection, so as to endanger that higher spiritual life, of which even then she was conscious. But He who had loved her with an everlasting love, and who well knew how perilous a snare this would prove to her, was pleased to lay her on a bed of sickness, and thus to withdraw her from the scene of danger and temptation. This was, I think, in the year 1821.

Then followed a period of much seclusion and bodily distress, from the continuance of feeble health. Her views, too, became clouded and confused, through an introduction to religious controversy, and the disturbing influence of various teachers, who held inadequate notions of the efficacy of Divine grace. She became deeply conscious of the evil in her own heart, and having not yet fully realised the fulness and freeness of the grace of God in the Lord Jesus Christ, she suffered much mental distress, under the painful uncertainty whether it were possible that such an one as she felt herself to be could be saved.

At this conjuncture it pleased God graciously to provide for her a spiritual teacher fully adapted to her necessities. It was an era in her life never to be forgotten. On the 9th of May, 1822, she was for the first time introduced to Dr. Cæsar Malan, of Geneva, in her father's residence, Grove House, Clapham, through the kind intervention of Miss Waddington, afterwards the wife of Bishop Shirley. From that time, for forty years, his constant correspondence was justly esteemed the greatest blessing of her life. The anniversary of

that memorable date was always kept as a festal
day; and on that day, so long as Dr. Malan lived,
commemorative letters passed from the one to the
other, as upon the birthday of her soul to true
spiritual life and peace.   The tenor of these com-
munications may be justly estimated from a letter
written about a fortnight after their first interview,
of which the following is a translation :—

MANCHESTER: *May 18th,* 1822.

" VERY DEAR FRIENDS,

"Since the Lord our God, our Saviour
and our Father, has deigned to make me 'find
favour in your eyes,' and since the word of His
minister has been agreeable and precious to you,
I can in peace and confidence continue to discuss
with you those things which belong to our eternal
salvation.

"The love of the Lord is over all His works :
His compassion is higher than the heavens.   He
forgets not any of His promises.   He is faithful.
We do not believe it, dear friends; our hearts
can neither imagine nor admit the *love* which God
bears us, unless they have been changed, renewed,
turned again unto the Lord by the powerful grace
of God.   Even in the Christian world, amongst those

who speak most freely of religion, the sentiment least found, and most seldom seen, is the simple, sincere consciousness of the love of God. One may converse for hours on the Gospel, or Church business; or discourse with learning and spirituality on some high doctrine, or question of morals, and thus may have it said, nay, even persuade ourselves, that there has been much edification in such and such a visit, or social gathering, or public service; and, nevertheless, remain as far from the life of God as are the men of the world in their calculations and vain pursuits.

"Dear friends, one look, silent but continuous and faithful at the cross of Jesus, is better, is more efficacious than all beside. It, at least, connects us with eternity; it is a look of life, aye, of life Divine. To say to oneself that the Lord loves us, that He is *our Father*, that He cherishes us, that He sees, follows, guides, guards us; to believe, but to believe *indeed*, that Jesus is our friend each day, each hour; that His grace surrounds us, that His voice continually bids us be happy and holy in Him; to dwell, child-like, in the joy of that love, and to repeat to one's soul, 'O my soul, my soul, dwell thou in peace, and bless thy God:'— all this which is life, and without which there is no life, either here below, or in the world above, is not the work of our own will; it is the direct achievement of the merciful and freely given power of Him who is 'over all, God blessed for ever;' who is love, and who desires to be called and recognized as the Father of infinite compassion.

"But, dear, truly dear friends and sisters, in our vanity, in frivolous presumption, in foolish error, we may flatter ourselves that we live, without this life; that we are wise, though ignorant of this truth; that we are content, happy, peaceful in the midst of our own agitation and in a path we try to trace in the quicksand of our glory, of the approbation of acquaintances, of our sciences, our lectures, our pleasures, etc. Then (and then very happily, Charlotte!) there is no more peace for an immortal soul thus deceived, bound, tenfold vanquished by the craft and seductions of Satan, of the world, of its own folly. For such a soul there are only bitter restlessness, long feebleness, tears, regrets, and continual sighings after a life it cannot attain, yet of which it feels the imperative need.

"But Jesus remains the same above this gloomy

ignorance, this culpable wandering: Jesus whose name is Saviour, Jesus who does not watch a wretched soul to condemn and destroy it, but to draw it to Himself, and to restore its life by pardoning all; Jesus looks upon this soul, and the dear soul is astonished to feel once more, to find repentant tears, and hope of grace and pardon, and joys which it had thought never to know again. Jesus looks upon Peter, and Peter can at last say, ' *Thou knowest* that I love Thee.'

"Ah, well! my very dear friends, since such a look has lighted on your beloved souls, since to-day you can say, 'We have found the Messiah,' and can rejoice in the light of His countenance, remain in that glorious possession while remaining *single-minded*, and only occupying yourselves, especially during these early days, with this consecration, with this joy: oh leave, I pray you in the name of your Redeemer, of your King who desires to reign over your *whole* heart, leave Martha's occupations, and be happy to sit tranquil at the feet of the Saviour, listening to what He has to tell you.

" Dear Eleanor, offer to Christ a sacrifice, a whole sacrifice,—do not keep back any part of your heart. Dear Charlotte, cut the cable, it will take too long to unloose it; cut it, it is a small loss; the wind blows and the ocean is before you —the Spirit of God, and eternity.

" Your brother and friend,

" C. MALAN."

Dr. Malan, as a skilful spiritual physician, had carefully probed the wound, and led her to the true remedy for all her anxiety,—namely, simple faith in God's own Word, directing her attention to such passages as the following: "Ho, every one that thirsteth, come ye to the waters, and he that hath no money; come ye, buy, and eat; yea, come, buy wine and milk without money and without price."[1] And again: "God so loved the world, that He gave His only begotten Son, that whosoever believeth in Him should not perish, but have everlasting life."[2] And again: "He that hath the Son hath life."[3] Whilst he thus showed her the fulness and freeness of this blessed Gospel, He also, with his own peculiar earnestness and tenderness, impressed upon her the guilt of " making God a liar by refusing to believe the record that He hath given of His Son."[4]

---

[1] Isa. lv. 1.
[3] 1 John v. 12.
[2] John iii. 16.
[4] 1 John. v. 10.

The Spirit of God accompanied his teaching.
The burden was lifted off that weary spirit; and
from that ever memorable day, my beloved sister's
spiritual horizon became for the most part cloud-
less. It is true that the suffering body would at
times weigh down her soul to the dust; but no
doubt ever again assailed her. Her faith never
was shaken. She might shrink from present suffering, or from unknown imagined terrors as to the
circumstances of her dying hour. But all beyond
was light and joy. Her constant testimony was:
" I know whom I have believed, and am persuaded
that He is able to keep that which I have committed unto Him against that day." [1]

Previous to the time of Dr. Malan's visit, my
sister's reading had been very discursive. The
noblest earlier writers in our own language, and
especially our poets, were her unceasing delight.
And all the best specimens of modern literature
were devoured with avidity as they appeared.
Dr. Malan at once perceived the spiritual danger
of such pursuits, so eagerly followed, to one of her
temperament. Under his advice, she threw aside
for a time the authors that she had found most

---

[1] 2 Tim. i. 12.

attractive, and confined herself to the exclusive study of Holy Scripture.

The result fully proved the wisdom of this advice. The blessed truths of the Bible laid hold on her mind irresistibly. She found there a more satisfying and elevating exercise for her thoughts, than in the highest efforts of human genius. The graphic power of the historical and biographical narratives, the dissection of character, the full development of Divine providence in all, created an interest in her mind that she had never equally experienced from the ordinary histories of mankind. Then the drapery, too, the brilliant imagery, the word painting, the rich orientalism of the poetry, and the colouring of the whole, so rich, and yet ever so true to nature, surpassed in her estimation all human compositions.[1] But, above all, she found the words of this holy Book speak with such power to her own soul, so accurately dissect her inmost thoughts, reveal to her so

---

[1] I find these lines written in her own private Bible:

"*Dig deep* in this precious golden mine,
Toil, and its richest ore is thine ;
Search, and the Saviour will lend His aid
To draw its wealth from its mystic shade:
Strive, and His Spirit will give thee light
To work in this heavenly mine aright.
Pray without ceasing, in Him confide,
Into all *truth* His light will guide."

clearly the dealings of God with herself, so fully set before her her own interest in the free grace of the blessed Saviour, that from that time forth to the end of life it was her principal study, her most delightful companion, and by day and by night her most unceasing meditation. She could say, as few others could, "The law of Thy mouth is better to me than thousands of gold and silver, sweeter also than honey and the honeycomb." And thus it was that she was prepared for that office which in later life devolved upon her for more than twenty-five years, the editing of the "Christian Remembrancer Pocket - Book;" the daily texts for which were for so long a time chosen by herself, and carefully arranged to illustrate the particular series of spiritual subjects which in each year she thought fit to select.

From this time her poetical talents became consecrated to religion ; and though she had in earlier years composed humourous poems, which were much admired by competent judges, she willingly renounced the *éclat* which this style of writing secured, and counting those things but loss which once were gain, devoted all the efforts of her pen henceforward to one object—the glory of God, and the benefit of others.

During many succeeding years, the personal intercourse with Dr. Malan was not unfrequent. For although his home was in Geneva, he visited England from time to time, and never without renewing his converse with those to whom his ministry had been so singularly beneficial.

It pleased God also about this period (1823), that many family illnesses and bereavements occurred, which deeply affected my beloved sister, and gave occasion to some of her most beautiful poems which appear in "The Hours of Sorrow."

During the autumn of the year 1823, an urgent invitation was received from Miss Waddington and her brother, asking my two sisters, with my brother Henry, to pay them a visit at St. Remy, in Normandy, their family estate. As the change was thought likely to benefit our dear invalid, arrangements were made at once for the journey to France, our brother Henry, who was tenderly attached to her, becoming the escort. She greatly enjoyed the novelty of French society and customs, and the foreign air agreed with her so well, that she felt equal to visit Paris before returning home. In November the travellers came back to Brighton, refreshed in mind and invigorated in bodily health.

During the following year, much occurred that was full of interest to my sister. A District Society was formed under the supervision of Mrs. Fry and the Rev. Edward Irving, who became our guests. Mrs. Fry was peculiarly attracted by my sister's character; and a warm friendship from this time was formed between them, which lasted through life. In some respects they were kindred spirits, each having experienced trial, and its blessed and refining influences.

About this time, also, we had a circle of very superior and delightful friends, most of them visitors for a time at Brighton. I may mention amongst those most valued and loved, the Cunningham family, Mr. Levison Gower and family, Mr. Owen of the Bible Society, Archdeacon and Mrs. Hoare, Dr. Macneile, the Wilberforces, and the family of Mr. and Mrs. Money. Though my sister was unable usually to join our family party when these guests were with us, she greatly enjoyed their converse in her own private room.

During the next three or four years, there does not occur to my memory much to record. Each winter was to her one of confinement and suffering; and when summer weather arrived, visits were made in various directions. But her health gave way entirely in 1829, and she became too weak to leave her room. In the following summer, it was thought that travelling, and entire change of air and scene and medical treatment, might prove of the greatest benefit. Arrangements were, therefore, made for her leaving home. She was so weak at the time that it was necessary to have her carried down-stairs and lifted into the carriage. A sister and a maid accompanied her, first into Devonshire, and then, in October, to Leamington, where she was at once placed in the hands of Dr. Jephson, a most skilful physician, and one who, from his discernment and intellectual character, was especially qualified to be useful to my sister, acting upon her body, as she often said, through her mind and understanding.

There we remained till the following May, Dr. Jephson proving as successful a physician for the body as Dr. Malan had been for the soul. Very gradually from this time my sister's habits of life were greatly changed. At the cost of much daily self-denial, earlier hours were adopted, and a diet strictly according to rule, with gentle walking exercise. Her state of mind at this period is illustrated by the following letter (written after our father's death):

SHIRLEY: *Nov. 12th*, 1833.

"To-morrow is your birthday, my Eleanor, and it is the second passed by you in a state of suffering, and after a bereavement which has made so affecting an alteration in our lives. I would, if it were possible, feel more tender sympathy and offer more earnest prayers on your behalf than I have ever done before, and infuse into these poor lines such balm and consolation as your own dear affection and sympathy have often dropped sweetly on my suffering heart.

"I would tell you also, my love, that though I did hope that your path would lie through a brighter and more flowery region than mine, yet even in the vale of suffering there are blessed companions to associate with—sweet consolations to partake of, heavenly privileges to enjoy. For myself, I am well content to tread it, and to remain in it, till my weary feet stand on the brink of Jordan.

> ' It costs me no regret that she
> Who followed Christ, should follow me;
> And though, where'er she goes,
> Thorns spring spontaneous at her feet,
> *I love her, and extract a sweet*
> E'en from my bitterest woes.'
> (*Madame Guion's " Address to Sorrow.*")

But I have been many years learning this difficult lesson,—and even now am but little skilled in this blessed alchemy.

"During the last few months, I humbly trust I have made some little progress, and oh! that what I have been taught by my heavenly Physician might be of some benefit to a sister I so tenderly love! Oh how many bitter tears have I shed for this cause, my Ellen; how many hard struggles and apparently fruitless ones, has it cost me to become resigned to this appointment of my heavenly Father; but *the struggle is over now.* He knows, and He alone, what it is, day after day, hour after hour, to fight against bodily feelings of almost overpowering weakness and languor and exhaustion; to resolve, as He enables me to do, not to yield to the slothfulness and the self-indulgence, the depression, the irritability such a body causes me to long to indulge,—but to rise every morning, determined on taking this for my motto: 'If any man will come after me, let him deny himself, take up his cross daily, and follow me;' and I trust He has made me willing to do this, and has also made the sorrows and sufferings of my earthly life the blessed means of detaching my heart from the love of it, and of giving me a longing, which seems each day to grow stronger, only to be made meet for my great change, to be sanctified wholly in body, soul, and spirit. And during these weeks and months of separation from my nearest friends, of seclusion and quietness, external and internal, much has been passing, my Ellen, between my soul and God,—such peace has been habitually granted to me,—such a sense of pardoning love,— such a bright hope that He has indeed chosen and accepted me, and is preparing me for His heavenly glory, refining and purifying me, that I shall ever remember this period as one of the happiest seasons of my life. The absence of agitation, and excitement, and bustle, the unbroken hours of reading and prayer, have been very helpful to me ; the very feeling of being a passing guest—an unimportant and solitary person in the family—has been useful to me, and has led me to draw nearer to God as my only and all satisfying portion."

In 1834 we became acquainted with Miss Harriet Kiernan, of Dublin, who came to England by medical advice, though, alas! too late to arrest the progress of fatal consumption. She became our loved guest before going to the Isle of Wight for the winter, and a most warm friendship was established from this time with our whole family, but more especially with our Charlotte. It was in compliance with her very earnest request, as a sort of dying legacy, that my sister undertook the editorship of the Christian Remembrancer Pocket-Book, which till this year had been in the hands of Miss Kiernan. During a period of twenty-five years, strength and ability were granted her to pre-pare annually the little volume, though few knew how much painful effort this editorship cost her. It was enriched by very careful selections from private MSS. and letters, and by many of her own original poems,—so that the sale increased wonder-fully, and a considerable sum was in consequence sent yearly towards the funds of a charitable insti-tution in Dublin (founded by the Miss Kiernans). For my sister always considered as *consecrated* money any profits that might accrue from any of her printed volumes, and to the close of her life would never appropriate any portion of it to her own use.

It was in this year that Miss Kiernan, in her last illness, had prepared a hymn-book for invalids, but it was little known or inquired for. The Rev. Hugh White, an unknown personal friend, but a valued correspondent of my sister, who began life as an officer in the army, but afterwards entered into Holy Orders, much desired to have this book revised; and in consequence, the present well-known volume, called "The Invalid's Hymn-Book," was arranged by my sister, with the addition of one hundred and twelve original hymns composed by herself, and prefaced by Mr. White. In a very short time the sale increased, and it now has reached the eighteenth thousand. In it was *first* published the widespread hymn, which has since been translated into French, Italian, and German :

> " Just as I am, without one plea
> But that Thy blood was shed for me,
> And that Thou bidd'st me come to Thee,
> O Lamb of God, I come!"

A young lady friend was so struck with it, that she had it printed as a leaflet and widely circulated, without any idea by whom it had been composed. It happened rather curiously that while we were living at Torquay, our valued Christian physician came to us one morning, having in his hand this leaflet. He offered it to my sister, saying, " I am sure this will please you ;" and great indeed was his astonishment at finding that it was written by herself, though by what means it had been thus printed and circulated she was utterly ignorant. Shortly after we became acquainted with the lady who had printed it.

In 1835 her health was so far restored, that she

yielded to the earnest request of some attached Scotch friends that she would pay them a visit at Dalgetty Manse. She travelled slowly by road the whole distance, and to her poetic eyes and imagination the Scotch scenery was full of charms. In reference to this journey she writes: "After Doncaster all the country was new to me; we had delightful weather and great enjoyment. Durham Castle and the Palace, from the bridge, have left a picture in my memory, as they stood out in fine antique relief, with the grey tint of time and its ivy upon them. Otherwise, till we entered Scotland, there was little to make any impression, but that which cultivated and undulating country, seen under a bright sun in fine weather, will always produce.

"When we crossed the Tweed, and entered the land I have so long loved and so often thought of, and so earnestly desired to visit, I felt sensations of unusual delight, blended with heartfelt gratitude to Him who, even in this our brief earthly pilgrimage, provides for us, and delights to bestow, so many varied enjoyments and sweet refreshments. Our friends contrived that I should enter Scotland by a road rich in beauty and in objects of interest. The silvery transparent Tweed, its richly-wooded banks, the fine seats embosomed in wood around it, with the beautiful range of the Pentland Hills, far more beautiful than our favourite Malvern,—all these things woke up feelings that long had slept in my bosom ; and often and often the tear of rapture started to my eye, as 'above, around, and underneath,' every object seemed to touch some responsive chord within, and to draw my heart towards Him 'without whom nothing that is made was made, and for whose pleasure all things are and were created.' How much is our delight in His exquisite works increased by our growing acquaintance with Him as our Creator, Father, Saviour, Mediator, Sanctifier, Comforter ; and how often as I looked at the glorious firmament, the hills, the woods, the waters, the cattle, all reposing in their beauty so peacefully, the words came to my mind, 'All Thy works praise Thee, and Thy saints bless Thee ! They show the glory of Thy kingdom and talk of Thy power, that Thy power, Thy glory, and the mightiness of Thy kingdom might be known unto men.' . . In spite of almost wintry weather, cold winds and rains, your sister feels herself so completely blest and happy, with such a sense of the Divine benediction resting upon her, that I think the actual vision of my blessed and only Saviour, and the actual sound of His own voice, saying, '*I am with thee*, My presence shall go with thee, and give thee rest,' could not exceed in certainty and sweet assurance the conviction I now feel, that in this place, and at this time, He does deal thus graciously with my soul."

Other thoughts and feelings, written the same year, find expression in the following letter:

"WESTFIELD LODGE, BRIGHTON:
"*April 11th*, 1835.

" You will receive this on the sweet day of rest, my beloved one, the day of nearest and fullest access to that King of Glory, who is ever ready to listen to us, and to grant all our petitions, if it be for His glory and our real good, that they shall be granted. May it be a day of refreshment and holy joy to my beloved companion, with whom, in spirit, I feel so closely, so inseparably united! 'Our bodies may far off remove, but still we're joined in heart;' and I find myself hour by hour, all day long, thinking of you, referring to you, talking of you, and most tenderly cherishing your remembrance within my heart. To-day I am thinking of your journey, and rejoicing in the beautiful gleams of vernal sunshine, and the sweet spring feeling in the air, which will, I trust, make travelling very pleasant, notwithstanding the number of little people and great people contained in the chariot, rendering it, perhaps, close and crowded. Oh, how much I wish I could really look upon all the painful incidents and circumstances of daily life, as only the passing unimportant annoyances of a journey,—a journey of which I trust far the larger part is accomplished, of which but a few short stages remain,—the one object I would bear in mind is its rapidly approaching termination.

> ' May I but safely reach *my home*,
> My God, my *heaven*, my *all*.'

"If I am weary on my way; 'in heaviness' through bodily suffering; or harassed by the scenes I witness around me, in these fearful times, how tranquillising is the thought, that none of these things can for a moment impede my homeward progress; nay, that they are designed to quicken it, and will assuredly do so, if sanctified to me as they may be by the word of God and prayer, and that I shall ere long leave a world 'made up of perturbations,' for that better country, in which now by faith I spend the only very happy hours

36

of my existence. Is it not, my beloved, exactly in proportion as we thither 'continually ascend,' and with our risen Lord habitually dwell, then that we find rest to our souls,—that we feel they have attained their proper centre ?"

One of the most striking features in my sister was her deep sympathy in all cases of sorrow or distress that were brought before her. It was a most tender and active sympathy, for willingly she would never refuse any application for pecuniary assistance,—indeed, her charities often exceeded her means.

Another marked feature was her habit of intercessory prayer, not only for all her relations, but for friends far off and near, especially those who might be in sorrow or suffering. Our noble Societies were never forgotten by her : the Bible Society, the Church Missionary, and the Jewish Society had special days of remembrance.

Towards the close of the year 1836 she was very ill, and some fears were entertained of serious disease. Happily, however, this was not the case ; but the advice of two eminent London surgeons led to the decision that entire change and travelling on the Continent would be most desirable.

Accordingly arrangements were made at once for the journey, and the months thus spent she always looked back upon as the most enjoyable of her whole life.

In November she returned to Brighton, after spending a short time at Tuxford vicarage, with our brother Edward, after his second marriage. And in 1836, while staying with the Venn family at Hereford, she writes :—

" I am sitting all alone in a pleasant little sitting room upstairs. I have that oppressive sense of heat and fulness which thunder-storms generally produce in me; a soft copious rain is falling around, with which I think thunder and lightning have been mingled. The sky is of that deep purplish grey which forms so rich a background to the bright green foliage ; and that stillness is prevailing which generally precedes thunder, as if Nature in humble silence did homage to Him ' whose voice shaketh terribly the earth.'

" I breakfasted most happily alone, with a blessed book in my hand, feeding my soul at the same time with my body. Since that time, I have been reading in that inexhaustible treasury of heavenly wisdom and comfort, the beautiful 3rd of Revelation, with its references in sweet Mrs. Shedden's

Bible, and have much enjoyed my noontide hour of intercessory prayer for all the dear ministers of Christ, and all the flocks committed to their charge, especially those connected with ourselves, and preparing for the holy Sabbath, and all my own beloved family, among whom I thought of thee, my love, and felt it sweet to pray for every blessing, spiritual and temporal, needed by thee, and known to be needed at this time by Him in whom we are, I trust, for ever united by a tie still dearer than that of any earthly relationship !

"Well, then, I set myself diligently to transcribe a paper of three sides of writing, for our Pocket-Book ("The Christian Remembrancer") which were needed. They are on the character of our Saviour, and will, I trust, be blessed to many to whom He is precious. From Bowdler and Tersteegen I have selected enough for the manuscript ; and now I am going to compose a few sacred lines to insert between the two papers, which will be a refreshing change of employment, as I have been writing for two hours. I have been walking about for a little exercise, and composed the lines I wished, which I think you will like (my own sister) when you see them in our Pocket-Book. The text I took for my motto is 2 Cor. iii. 18 ; and, if I do not deceive myself, they were from my heart, as well as my pen. Oh ! how sweet it is to strive to do every-thing in the name and to the glory of such a Lord and Master, and to be permitted in everything to ask His aid, and to aspire to His blessed approbation.

"It is delightful to me at all times to be alone, when I can employ myself; though, as you well know (by having at such times been my sweet cheerer and comforter), there are periods and feel-ings which utterly disable me, and then perfect solitude is heavy. Since I have been here I have had only enough of it to enjoy, and to strive I hope to improve. But I dwell upon the thought more and more, that our earthly life is only a short journey, some of its stages wearisome and long, perhaps, but not one that does not carry us nearer to our home; and, blessed be God, not one that is not cheered by His presence, and passed through under His gracious direction; and while these are granted, the soul is happy, and even joyful, though she feels the burden and the clog of a suffering mortal frame. My own *mental* comfort, I own, almost surprises me, so constant even here is the sense of bodily weariness and indisposition; but the sweet hope, almost amounting to conviction, that all is and will be well with me ultimately, that my light affliction which is but for a moment, is working out even for me an exceeding and eternal weight of glory, this carries me cheerfully on. And, as I do believe my humble prayer will be answered more and more, by the peaceable fruits of righteousness being formed in me, that so before I go hence and am no more seen, my Saviour may really be glorified in my body and spirit which are His, I am not only willing but thankful to suffer, because I believe that it is to make me a partaker of His holiness.

"I look on at these diligent fellow-labourers spending so many hours every day in labours of love among the ignorant and wretched, which I am unable to share, and then I remember Milton's sweet lines, 'They also serve who only stand and wait;' and again I remember with comfort how short that waiting time may be for me."

We left home for Dover on June 27, 1837, a brother-in-law being our kind escort. We travelled by post, through the north of France, to Brussels and Frankfort, and so on to Basle; just stopping where there were objects of interest, or excellent ministers to whom Dr. Steinkopff had given us introductions. Our weather was lovely, and greatly did the novelty and variety exhilarate and delight my beloved sister, especially the Rhine scenery.

After reaching Geneva, we felt at once in the midst of friends : our intercourse with Dr. Malan was renewed; and, in addition, we had the delightful society of Professor Gaussen and his daughter, with whom we made a short tour through the Bernese Oberland. The Alpine scenery, and the mountain air, seemed to give new life to our dear invalid. Chamounix and the Mer de Glace were visited in company with Dr. Malan ; and so much was she invigorated that we ventured the ascent of Montanvert to see the glorious sunrise over the Mer de Glace, at four o'clock in the morning. She went in a *chaise à porteur*, while I mounted a horse, and rode with Dr. Malan. In after years, when speaking of this tour, she thus writes to a Scotch friend who was travelling in Switzerland :

"Yes, my beloved J., the feelings of delight and wonder, and adoring gratitude and praise, excited by the scenes around you, can never be imagined even, much less realised, till the enraptured eye beholds them ! and how truly do I participate in your counting all the splendid achievements in the palaces of Versailles, and the magnificence of Paris, as mere baubles and worthless toys, in comparison with the matchless works of our glorious Creator. To me, those mountains and emerald valleys, and rivers and waterfalls, awakened such exquisite sensations of delight, as I never expect to experience again, till I shall gaze upon the new heavens and the new earth, in still sweeter society, and with an outward frame more suited to them than this feeble mortal body;—though I felt on those heights as if I had already dropped the garments of mortality!"

Late in October we returned home, crossing the Jura mountains, and so through France to Boulogne, her health and spirits greatly invigorated.

I think it was some time in this year that the little volume called "Hymns for a Week," was first privately printed, to assist the funds of a Bazaar held at Brighton, for St. Mary's Hall. Surreptitious copies of these hymns were afterwards circulated and sold by an individual who claimed them as his own composition! This obliged the real authoress to have the book published with her name, and it has now reached the fortieth thousand.

During the next two or three years there does not occur much to record. The winters were always more or less suffering; and in the summer months visits were made in various directions—to Torquay, Leamington, and Shirley.

In 1841 the death of a most beloved sister-in-law, Mrs. Henry Elliott, crushed her to the earth ; and this blow was followed by our mother's fatal illness in 1842. She was taken from us in April, 1843, and thus our Brighton home was broken up. It was during these last years that some of the most touching poems in "The Hours of Sorrow" were composed. Two sisters also passed away in the following year; so that to a frame already much enfeebled, the effect of these successive shocks was very distressing ; and she became so alarmingly ill, from some attack in the heart, that an immediate change of scene was imperative.

It was at this time, when she thought it probable she could not recover, that the following fragmentary letter, dated August, 1843, addressed to her brother Henry and her sister Eleanor, was written, though it was never discovered till 1871, after she had safely landed on the heavenly shore.

*   *   *   "When this paper meets your eyes our sweet relationship will have closed for ever ; but will our union be broken, our connection dissolved, because my poor suffering body is laid in the grave, and my spirit has returned to God who gave it? Oh! my beloved companions and counsellors, it will only be exchanged for a better, and more intimate, and more perfect union—for an eternal relationship; and I shall be fitter for your love, and better adapted for your society, when you read these lines, which I water with my tears, than I have ever been while imprisoned in a body of sin and death, and mourning unceasingly over all my countless faults and inconsistencies.

"I humbly hope, nay, I hope it is not presumptuous to say, that I rejoicingly *believe*, I shall then be 'without spot, before the throne of God and of the Lamb,—and the days of my mourning will be ended.' Therefore, my precious brother, my own beloved sister, 'weep not for me.' Think of me as for ever safe, for ever pardoned, for ever holy, for ever happy through the blood of the everlasting covenant, and the unspeakable mercy of Him who 'hath loved me with an everlasting love.' From that love I am persuaded nothing will ever separate me; nothing I may still have to endure in life,— nothing I may be called to pass through in death. I have fled for refuge to the hope set before the vilest of sinners! In my earliest childhood I dis-

tinctly remember feeling the drawing of my heavenly
Father to His beloved Son, the Lord Jesus Christ;
and in my often wayward youth His Spirit never
ceased to strive with me, convincing me of sin,
and making me miserable under the sense of it,
and my only gleams of happiness were" (here the
fragment closes abruptly).

In consequence of her increased illness, our
beloved brother, the Rev. Henry Venn Elliott,
who was very tenderly attached to his sister,
arranged for us a journey into Devonshire under
his escort. Linton and Lynemouth and Ilfra-
combe were the places chosen; and again the
total change of scene, with the varied beauties of
that lovely neighbourhood into which she so fully
entered, proved very reviving to her shattered
frame. After a time she rallied so much that we
ventured to return to Brighton, though Westfield
Lodge was to be no longer our home, but a pleasant house in Regency Square, where we remained
during the chief part of the following year.

Early in the spring of 1845 we were again
advised to spend some months on the Continent;
and, accordingly, we sailed from London to
Antwerp in May. My sister had intended wintering
with me in Italy; but illness obliged us to return

home in July. Later in that year we moved to
Torquay by medical advice; and there, during
fourteen years, we found a delightful and beautiful
home, which my sister greatly loved and enjoyed.
The exquisite scenery just suited her poetical taste;
and though she was again and again confined to
the house by illness, she was never weary of feast-
ing her eyes on the lovely landscape spread before
her windows. Many choice friends visited us
during these years; amongst those specially valued
were the late Archdeacon Hodson and Rev. W.
Cleaver, who often kindly arranged to come on
the Sunday to administer the sacrament, and thus
to compensate in a measure by their ministrations
her privation in being unable to attend the public
services in which she so delighted.

The editorship of "The Christian Remembrancer
Pocket-Book" occupied much of her time, particu-
larly in the consecutive arrangement of the daily
texts, which varied according to the special subjects chosen for each year. This employment she
delighted in, and often hours would be spent in
what we called smilingly her "gold diggings."

In 1857 circumstances combined to make it
advisable to try the effect of a more bracing
climate; and having two brothers, with their

families, settled at Brighton, we determined once
more to return to that place endeared by so many
early associations. Accordingly, the change was
made; and my sister's life was prolonged for fourteen years, during which period she was continually engaged in preparing the Pocket-Book,
and in composing many additional hymns and
poems as circumstances arose either of joy or
sorrow to call out her tender interest and sympathy. Some weeks during the summer months
were usually passed in the country. At Tunbridge
Wells she greatly enjoyed the drives, and the
occasional society of many friends; and certainly
she became stronger after we left Torquay, though
advancing age gradually occasioned increasing
feebleness. Still she was able, when at Brighton,
to enjoy the pleasures of intellectual and spiritual
society; and her zest and delight in reading herself,
or in listening to others, continued as fresh and
lively as ever, almost to the close of life!

During the latter end of her life it was her constant habit before closing her eyes at night, and
immediately on first waking in the morning, to
repeat to herself certain verses chosen as most
suitable for these special seasons, and which she
always called her morning and evening "ladder."

—I think it was like Jacob's ladder between earth and heaven !

The death of our beloved brother Henry, in January, 1865, was a crushing blow, and rendered more deeply painful because of her inability to go to him, even to bid him a last farewell ; for she was at that time entirely confined to the house and often to her bed. On the last birthday he spent on earth she addressed to him the following touching and characteristic letter :

"MY DARLING BROTHER,—I send *three* little mites for your *three* charitable funds, with 'a willing mind,' and a grateful heart; and may the privilege be granted to me of helping you in some little measure, by my poor but heartfelt prayers, in all the arduous works entrusted to you by your heavenly Master, and in which, indeed, you have long 'laboured and have not fainted.' Oh, how full has my heart been of deep and loving thoughts of *you*, my brother, on *this* day; and how sweet and precious to me has the privilege been of pouring out all these thoughts to Him whose you are, for whom you labour, and who says to you, ' Be thou faithful unto death, and I will give thee a crown of life.' You feed *His* sheep, my Henry,—

you feed *His* lambs ; and when the chief Shepherd shall appear, what an abundant recompense will He bestow. I have asked three things especially for my darling brother on this day :—*First :* that his eye may be single, and his whole body full of light, and his path as ' the shining light, which shineth more and more unto the perfect day.'— *Secondly :* that God may prosper all His work of faith and patience, of hope and labour of love, both in dear St. Mary's Hall and in St. Mary's congregation, for every one of whom I try to pray. —*Thirdly :* for strength of body equal to your need, to be granted, and some helper found, to lighten the burden which is too heavy for you ; and for such peace to fill your soul, that nothing may harass you, and every trial may be turned into a blessing. These are the prayers continually offered for my precious brother from the heart of his much-indebted and most loving sister (now in her feeble old age), C. E."

Her attachment to this brother was most deep and tender ; and, as he was younger than herself, she had always hoped and expected that he would minister to her in her dying hours ! But God had ordered otherwise ; and though, as she often said, his removal changed the aspect of her life, and was indeed an irreparable loss, yet it was very beautiful to notice her meek submission under the heavy chastisement, and to observe how she was enabled to say in the language of her own well-known hymn :

> What though in lowly grief I sigh
> For friends beloved no longer nigh;
> Submissive still would I reply,
>   " Thy will be done !"
>
> If Thou should'st call me to resign
> What most I prize, it ne'er was mine,
> I only yield Thee what was Thine :
>   " Thy will be done !"

The last time she was able to leave home was in 1867, when we spent some weeks at Keymer, a pretty quiet village within a drive from Brighton, and sheltered from the keen winds by the South Downs. The perfect quiet of this village, the pretty cheerful views from our window, with the soft balmy air proved very reviving and delightful. Indeed she rallied so much that she was able not only to take drives in the neighbourhood, but to walk in the garden, to sit in the verandah, and to watch the haymakers in their busy work in the adjoining fields. After our return to Brighton in the autumn her strength gradually lessened, so that we found it necessary to spare every exertion ;

from this time she never left the house, and was usually carried in a chair up and down stairs.

In the autumn of 1869 an acute inflammatory attack, attended with great suffering, so entirely reduced her remaining strength, that her medical friends had no hope of her rallying; and during two or three days those around watched by her bedside, almost doubting whether the heavy sleep was not the sleep of death! It was after this attack that she wrote the following hitherto unpublished verses:

Darling, weep not! I must leave thee,
  For a season we *must* part!
Let not this short absence grieve thee,
  We shall still be one in heart;
And a few brief sunsets o'er,
We shall meet to part no more!

Sweet has been our earthly union,
  Sweet our fellowship of love;
But more exquisite communion
  Waits us in our home above;
Nothing there can loose or sever
Ties ordained to last for ever.

Sweet has been thy tender feeling
  Through long years for this poor frame:
Love and care, like balm of healing,
  Have kept up life's feeble flame;
Now these dying pangs betoken
That the "silver cord" is broken.

Dearest! those sad features pain me:
  Wipe those loving tears away!
Let thy stronger faith sustain me,
  In this dark and cloudy day!
Be my "Hopeful," make me brave,
Lift my head above the wave!

Place me in those arms as tender,
  But more powerful far than thine :
For a while thy charge surrender
  To His guardianship divine !
Lay me on my Saviour's breast,
There to find eternal rest !

To the surprise of all, however, it pleased God
that she should yet remain with us a little longer ;
but from this period she was entirely confined to
her bed, only leaving it to rest on the couch for a
few hours. But even in this weak and suffering
state her mind continued clear, and her affections
as tender and fresh as ever. Her bedroom windows
looked over the country to the west ; and great
was her delight in observing the beautiful sunsets,
and all the varying colourings of the clouds,—she
even wished to be roused from sleep when there
was a rainbow, or any special beauty in the sky.
Her love for flowers was almost a passion ; and to
the last week of her life she would have the nose-
gays sent by loving friends on her bed, and arrange
them with her own peculiar and elegant taste.

In the last two years of her life, and especially
during the last few months, there was much increase of weakness and suffering ; but, amidst all,
the grace of our Lord Jesus Christ was hourly
magnified in her. Those at her side noted most
thankfully her sweet peace, her bright hope, her

gentle, humble, fearless drawing near to the gates
of death; her deep love of Scripture and rich enjoyment of its precious truths; her earnest resist-
ance to all error; her bringing all to the standard
of that Divine Word; her abiding love to the
name and the person of Jesus; her full trust, most
humbly, in His atoning merits and intercession;
her yearning after the hour when He would come
to take her to Himself; and yet her patience under
prolonged suffering; and her simple desire that
God would glorify Himself in her, living or dying,
doing or suffering His holy will. All is but as a
present, living, most blessed history to those who
survive, an earlier fragment of that which will be
fully developed in eternity. The principle of all was
simple reliance on the word and the work of Christ.
He had *done all for her*. He had *promised all to her*.

She was as the limpet on the rock (she would
often say), so clinging to her blessed Saviour, that
any effort to tear her from Him was like rending
her soul asunder; or, she was as the happy infant
on its mother's lap, with no strength, but needing
none; fully supported by those loving arms, and
only looking up to the beam of light and love
on that blessed countenance, when the sweetest
joy would steal into her soul.

Or again, she would retrace in her own mind all she had ever known or read of worth and beauty in man or nature,—all of genius and glory, the highest and best on earth,—all the loveliest and most noble characters that had ever evoked admiration or esteem. She would review them all, with a rich unfolding of the several pictures, and a comparison of them with the portraiture, in her own mind, of Him "in whom are hid all the treasures of wisdom and knowledge." She would speak of each one—Milton, Dante, Newton, St. Paul, etc.—as but a faint outline, a shadowy reflection, of His glorious excellency. And thus, when no one was by, in the silent hours of darkness, her solitary musings, of which she would give an account the following day, often made even wakefulness to be no weariness, and her sick chamber as the pavilion of her Saviour's presence.

As to material images or pictures, she felt that they did but cripple and confine her meditations, and draw them down to earth. And the pomp of a gorgeous ceremonial was to her but the attempt to create a semblance of religion, when the heart could not rise to the reality. Many years since, her living motto had been expressed in those simple lines :

Oh, Jesus, make Thyself to me
A living, bright reality,
More present to Faith's vision keen
Than any outward object seen,—
More dear, more intimately nigh,
Than e'en the sweetest earthly tie.

At one period, when her weakness made it no longer possible for her to attend the public sanctuary that she so dearly loved, this was the expression of her mind : "My Bible is my Church. It is always open, and there is my High Priest ever waiting to receive me. There I have my confessional, my thanksgiving, my psalms of praise, a field of promises, and a congregation of whom the world is not worthy—prophets and apostles, and martyrs and confessors—in short, all I can want I there find."

In the last years and days of her life—days of increased weakness and suffering—she was sustained and blessed with a sense of her Saviour's love and her Saviour's presence, and with a sure and abiding trust in Him.

In a private paper writen for her sister Eleanor, at the commencement of her 81st year, she says :—

"I feel that so great an age as mine requires three things—great faith, great patience, and great peace. Come what may during the year upon which we have entered, I firmly believe that goodness and mercy, like two guardian angels, will follow us during every day, in every hour, in every varying circumstance through which we may have to pass,—in every time of trouble sustaining and comforting us,—the angel of His presence keeping ever by our side, and whispering, Fear not, for I am with thee,—be not dismayed, for I am thy God. We may have to part for a short season with each other; but He has promised never, never to leave us,—never, never to forsake us."

When parting with another beloved sister, a few weeks before her death, she said,—"Our next meeting will be at the marriage-supper of the Lamb."

When the verse, "Let not your heart be troubled," was repeated to her, she quietly said, "But my heart is *not* troubled;" adding, "My mind is full of the Bible." And that word was her support when speech had failed her, and she was passing through the dark valley.

The last manifestation of consciousness was on the morning of her death, when, on her sister repeating to her their text for the day, "Thine eyes shall see the King in His beauty, they shall behold the land that is very far off," she clasped her hands together ; and as she raised her eyes to heaven, a beam came over her countenance, which showed that she fully entered into the precious words, and was realising the glorious vision she was so soon to behold. On the evening of that day, September 22nd, at 10 o'clock, without any apparent suffering, or the slightest struggle, she fell asleep in Jesus, so peacefully that it was difficult to fix the moment when the gentle breathing ceased.

Selections from the Poems

OF

CHARLOTTE ELLIOTT.

To a Fellow Traveller.

"Thou wilt keep him in perfect peace whose mind is stayed on
Thee, because he trusteth in Thee."

WHAT is our sweetest joy?
    Beloved companion! say;
What our delightful, best employ,
Untiring, free from all alloy,
    In this dark cloudy day?
To speak together of our home,
Looking for Him who soon will come.

Where do our spirits find
    Refreshment and repose?
When heart to heart, and mind to mind,
We search those records God designed
    To medicine all our woes;
And feel, as bright its pages shine,
Each line was traced by Love divine.

We look on all around
As soon to disappear;
We listen to the tempest's sound,
As wildly now it sweeps around,
Without an anxious fear;
We hear a voice amidst its swell
Which whispers—"All will soon be well!"

Yes, soon the Lord will come;
Then will all troubles cease;
Earth's kingdoms will His own become;
Proud antichrist will meet his doom,
All will be joy and peace:
These very storms prepare His way,
And usher in that glorious day.

The Comforter.

Spirit of truth, of power, of love,
Who mak'st the contrite heart Thy seat,
The Father's promise from above,
Blest Paraclete!

The gift by Christ sent down from heaven
  To cheer His flock, then tempest-tost,
The abundant compensation given
          For Him they lost;

Spirit! the Church's Comforter,
  With whom Thou deignest to abide,
Light, strength, and teaching to confer,
          Our steps to guide:

Spirit of Jesus! one with Him,
  And with the eternal Father one!
Remove the veil that renders dim
          That glorious Sun.

Oh manifest Thy power anew!
  Reveal His love, His truths divine!
Till in Thy light those truths we view,
          In vain they shine.

"Spirit of glory and of Christ!"
  Now lead us at His feet to fall;
Show us His ransom has sufficed;
          Make Him our all!

The Secure Refuge.

"Lead me to the Rock that is higher than I."—*Psalm* lxi. 2.

O Thou, the hope, the strength of Israel,
Their hiding-place, in which secure they dwell,
The rock round which the billows vainly chafe,
While hidden in its clefts, Thine own are safe.
Lo! tempest-tossed, bewildered, weary, weak,
That blessed hiding-place, my God, I seek.

I see the swelling tide advancing still;
A thousand fears my trembling bosom fill;
I stretch my hands, I lift my feeble cries;
On that safe spot I fix my straining eyes;
Oh now let Mercy's arm, with power divine,
Place me upon that rock, and take me in!

I see no other rock—no safe retreat;
Roughly the waves and storms around me beat;
A shipwrecked, houseless mariner I roam;
Earth has for me no resting-place, no home;
O sheltering rock! let me but safely hide
Within Thy clefts, I ask no boon beside!

Once sheltered there, for ever safe from fear,
The gathering storms I, undismayed, shall hear;
Once sheltered there, how will my heart rejoice
Beneath its shadow, listening to that Voice
Whose heavenly accents bid all trouble cease,
Control the winds and waves, and whisper peace.

I cast no " longing, lingering look behind;"
On life's rough ocean no repose I find;
I see it strewed with many a fearful wreck,
And many a gallant bark I vainly seek,
Which had 'they sought the rock, when tempest-
    tossed,
Would ne'er, 'mid shoals and quicksands, have been
    lost.

Here will I watch and wait, and " wish for day,"
O Rock of Ages! at Thy foot I stay!
Let not the dashing waves unclasp my hold!
Let Mercy's arms my trembling form enfold,
And place me where " Thy hidden ones " repose,
Till the new earth and heaven their charms disclose.

The Bridegroom Cometh.

"Blessed is he whom the Lord, when He cometh, shall find watching."

THOU for whom we look, now aid me
　　Still to watch, and trim my light!
Thou in white robes hast arrayed me,
　　I must watch to keep them white;
Cold without, rough winds are blowing,
　　And within the air falls damp;
Still amid the darkness glowing,
　　Bright must shine my bridal lamp.

Thy free grace, Thy love unbounded,
　　Chose, and bade me waiting stand,
Till the glad call should be sounded,
　　" Lo! the Bridegroom is at hand!"
Though the time seems long and dreary,
　　And the watch is hard to keep,
Still, though faint and weak and weary,
　　Lord! permit me not to sleep.

Let me watch for Thine appearing,
  Till the bridal pomp I hail;
Till, night's mists and shadows clearing,
  Streaming o'er the illumined vale
I discern the rising splendour,
  Catch from far their sweet acclaim,
Whose unnumbered voices render
  Praise and glory to Thy name!

Then, to swell the grand procession,
  May we haste without a fear!
While, enriched by our accession,
  Sweeter anthems greet Thine ear.
Then may my white robe be stainless—
  May my lamp shed light around!
E'en without a spot and blameless,
  May I at that hour be found!

Then the bride, indeed " made ready,"
  Shall be brought with joy untold;
Now no more defiled or needy,
  But in raiment of wrought gold.
For this hour the whole creation
  Groaned and travailed, as in birth—
Now the glorious consummation
  Fills with joy new heavens and earth.

The Daily Lesson.

"Lord, what wilt Thou have me to do?"—*Acts* ix. 6.

WHAT is the lesson I am taught
  Daily and hourly, Friend Divine?
O could I learn it as I ought!
  To have no will but Thine.

Oft I feel eager to fulfil
  Some right intent, as best I may;
Then comes the mandate "to be still,"
  To work not, but obey.

I meekly plead, "Life's little hour
  For me, far spent, will soon expire;"
My Lord replies, "Thou wilt have power
  When thou shalt come up higher."

In others, in myself, I see
  Evils I long at once to cure;
Then comes this gentle check to me;
  "Be patient, and endure."

I think, if this or that were changed,
   I could do better, and do more;
But is not every step arranged
   By Thee, whom I adore?

That wisdom which can never fail,
   That love whose depths can ne'er be scanned,
E'en in its most minute detail,
   My daily life has planned.

Then let me with implicit faith
   In Thee confide, on Thee depend,
And say, " Choose Thou my hourly path,
   E'en to the end."

Thoughts to Comfort.

I NEED no other plea
   With which to approach to God,
Than His own mercy, boundless, free,
   Through Christ on man bestowed ;
A Father's love, a Father's care,
Receives and answers every prayer.

I need no human ear,
In which to pour my prayer;
My Great High Priest is ever near,
On Him, I cast my care;
To Him, Him only, I confess,
Who can alone absolve and bless.

I need no works by me
Wrought with laborious care,
To form a meritorious plea
Why I heaven's bliss should share.
Christ's finished work, through boundless grace
Has there secured my dwelling-place.

I need no prayers to saints,
Beads, relics, martyrs' shrines;
Hardships 'neath which the spirit faints,
Yet still, sore burdened, pines;
Christ's service yields my soul delight,
Easy His yoke, His burden light.

I need no other book
To guide my steps to heaven,
Than that on which I daily look,
By God's own Spirit given;
And this when He illumes our eyes,
"Unto salvation makes us wise."

I need no holy oil
　To anoint my lips in death;
No priestly power my guilt to assoil,
　And aid my parting breath;
Long since those words bade fear to cease,
"Thy faith hath saved thee, go in peace."

I need no priestly mass,
　No purgatorial fires,
My soul t' anneal, my guilt to efface,
　When this brief life expires;
Christ died my eternal life to win,
His blood has cleansed me from all sin.

I need no other dress,
　I urge no other claim,
Than His unspotted righteousness;
　In Him complete I am;
Heaven's portals at that word fly wide,
No passport do I need beside.

The Christian Warrior.

WARRIOR! the foe is stirring and a-field,
   While thou art slumbering, he is broad awake;
Thou who art pledged to conquer, not to yield,
   Shouldst, ere the dawn, thy calm precautions take,

And reconnoitre all the hostile lines;
   A battle must be fought *this very day:*
Oh choose thy vantage ground—thwart his designs,
   Prepare to meet his terrible array!

His eye is fixed on each unguarded spot;
   There, at thy *weakest point*, he aims his force;
He plans thy ruin, plans and wearies not,
   To wiles and stratagems will have recourse.

Is this a time for slumber or for sleep?
   Is this a time for sloth's enticements bland?
Now, when thou'rt called unceasing watch to keep,
   And wait the onset, standing sword in hand.

Christian ! thy life is but a brief campaign ;
   Though hardships, conflicts, perils *must* be shared,
Fear not to meet them—transient is the pain,
   The victory certain—the reward prepared.

A Song in the Night.

"Looking unto Jesus."—*Heb.* xii. *2.*

JESUS, my Saviour! look on me,
   For I am weary and opprest;
I come to cast my soul on Thee :
         Thou art my rest.

Look down on me, for I am weak;
   I feel the toilsome journey's length ;
Thine aid omnipotent I seek :
         Thou art my strength.

I am bewildered on my way;
   Dark and tempestuous is the night;
Oh shed Thou forth some cheering ray !
         Thou art my light.

Why feel I desolate and lone?
  Thy praises should my thoughts employ;
Thy presence can pour gladness down :
    Thou art my joy.

When the accuser flings his darts
  I look to Thee—my terrors cease—
Thy cross a hiding-place imparts :
    Thou art my peace.

Vain is all human help for me ;
  I dare not trust an earthly prop ;
My sole reliance is on Thee :
    Thou art my hope.

Full many a conflict must be fought,
  But shall I perish, shall I yield?
Is that bright motto given for nought,
    " Thou art my shield ?"

Standing alone on Jordan's brink
  In that tremendous, latest strife,
Thou wilt not suffer me to sink :
    Thou art my life.

Thou wilt my every want supply
  E'en to the end, whate'er befall ;
Through life, in death, eternally,
    Thou art my all.

74

A Hymn of Praise.

LORD of the mountains, and the hills!
  Lord of the rivers, and the vales!
Thy glory all creation fills;
  Thy goodness all creation hails!

While these Thy works delight our eyes,
  So rich, diversified, and fair,
Let praise within our hearts arise,
  Let gratitude be glowing there.

Let Spring's fair promise, Summer's charms,
  Autumnal beauties, full and free,
Each Wintry hearth Thy kindness warms,
  Awake the song of praise to Thee.

Let the first blush of rosy light
  Call forth the consecrated strain!
Let silvery stars and moonbeams bright
  Wake the sweet melodies again!

While noontide zephyrs, breathing balm,
  Waft the rich scent of plant and flower,
Let praise 'mid adoration's calm,
  With the heart's incense fill the hour.

Let childhood's voice to Thee direct
  Its morning hymn, its evening thought;
Let manhood's ripened intellect
  To praise Thee all its powers devote.

And oh, when we have past away,
  When all *our* generation sleep,
Let those we train take up the lay,
  And with heaven's choir sweet concert keep!

The Path of the Just.

"The path of the just is as the shining light, that shineth more
and more unto the perfect day."

I VIEW an upward path of light,
Winding round many a beauteous height,
    And rising, rising still;
Till that resplendent spot be gained,
By mortal footstep ne'er attained;
    Zion's celestial hill.

Those who from thence the prospect hail,
First drop mortality's dark veil,
    And angel robes put on;
We, who have loved to track their way,
Just view them catch the ethereal ray;
    But while we gaze, they're gone.

Still they have left a golden line
Of heavenly radiance, which will shine
    Long, long to memory's eye;
Bidding us tread the path they trod
E'en till we share their bright abode,
    Their pure felicity.

The Fountain.

"In that day there shall be a fountain opened to the house of David
for sin and for uncleanness."—*Zech.* xiii. 1.

THERE is a fountain deep and pure,
    Forth from the riven rock it flows;
A healing spring and lasting cure
    For all terrestrial ills and woes.

Thither, each morning, leave I crave
 To take my feeble sin-sick soul—
Emerging from that cleansing wave
 Unspotted, vigorous, glad, made whole.

When faint with noon-day toil and heat,
 For comfort thither I repair;
Around it all is calm and sweet,
 Rest and refreshment greet me there.

And when the shadowy veil of night
 Across the dewy earth is spread,
And the pale moonbeam's silvery light
 Soft o'er the silent stream is shed;

Oh then, in that serenest hour,
 My purest, holiest joys are given;
Sin, sorrow, Satan, lose their power,
 Around me breathe the airs of heaven.

That Holy One Who deigned to heal
 One sufferer by Bethesda's pool,
There, while beside the fount I kneel,
 Himself draws near and makes me whole.

Thrice blessed fountain! when I reach
 The source from whence thy waters flow,
Then shall I praise, in fitter speech,
 That love to which such joys I owe.

A Meditation and Prayer.

" The secret things belong unto the Lord our God."
Deut. xxix. 29.

O GOD, my God, these aching thoughts control,
Still the deep restless yearnings of my soul,
In endless mazes of conjecture lost,
Bewildered, baffled, wearied, tempest-tost,
Striving in vain those clouds to penetrate,
Which hide my future, my eternal state.

Check these tumultuous thoughts, so strong, so wild;
Let me not be by Satan's snares beguiled;
The things revealed alone belong to man;
Why strive deep hidden mysteries to scan?
"Such knowledge is too wonderful for me;"
Lord ! as a little child I fain would be.

My restless soul ! what do those thoughts avail?
Why strive to pierce the impenetrable veil?
Alas ! thy faith amounts not yet to sight !
How should the finite grasp the infinite ?
How should an atom on this earthly ball
Search out the great First Cause. God over all ?

A Meditation and Prayer.

This present life is but my infancy;
Even the objects which around I see
Are full of secrets, still but little known,
Though earth's six thousand years some light have
But all beyond, vast, vast eternity,   [thrown.
Is veiled from man, an undiscovered sea!

None has returned from that mysterious bourne;
Millions have passed away, and those we mourn
Are living somewhere, but we know not where;
Faith only tells what blessedness they share;
And its bright lamp, hung o'er the gulf of night,
"Brings life and immortality to light."

They fell asleep in Jesus, they are blest;
This must suffice me, on this truth I rest;
But the bright marvels of that unknown shore,
As yet 'tis not permitted to explore;
But yet a little while and I shall know
(For God has said it) what I know not now.

"A meek and quiet spirit," this I ask;
Fulfilling daily my appointed task;
Sitting, like Mary, at the Master's feet,
Aiming at nothing high, at nothing great;
Content from Him all knowledge to receive,
Nor seeking more than He is pleased to give.

The Day is at Hand!

—•c•—

Poor fainting spirit, still hold on thy way,
        The dawn is near!
True, thou art weary; but yon brightening ray
        Becomes more clear.
Bear up a little longer—wait for rest—
Yield not to slumber, though with toil opprest.

The night of life is mournful—but look on—
        The dawn is near!
Soon will earth's shadowy scenes and forms be gone,
        Yield not to fear!
The mountain's summit will, ere long, be gained.
And a bright world of joy and peace attained.

"Joyful through hope" thy motto still must be;
        The dawn is near!
What glories will that dawn unfold to thee!
        Be of good cheer!
Gird up thy loins; bind sandals on thy feet;
The way is dark and long, the end is sweet.

C

Onward and Upward.

" My soul followeth hard after Thee."—*Psalm* lxiii 8.

I LOOK to Thee! I hope in Thee!
  I glory in Thy name!
I make Thy righteousness my plea,
  Thou all-atoning Lamb!
Methinks e'en death will welcome be,
That I, through death, may pass to Thee.

Though now but "darkly through a glass"
  Thy beauty I behold,
E'en the faint image I can trace
  Fills me with joy untold;
May I but catch one glimpse of Thee,
None, none beside I ask to see.

"Thou art my portion," saith my soul,
  My all in earth or heaven;
None but Thyself can make me whole,
  No name but Thine is given
At which the gates of pearl fly wide—
The passport of the justified.

I know Thy voice—I strive to keep
  Thy Word within my heart;
Though the most worthless of Thy sheep,
  Still Thou my Shepherd art;
Firm as a rock that word shall stand,
None, none shall pluck me from Thy hand.

"Without repentance are Thy gifts;"
  This thought my hope sustains,
In deep distress my soul uplifts,
  When sin the victory gains;
My faith, though weak, shall never fail;
Thy prayer shall e'en for me prevail.

When I Thy glory shall behold,
  And see Thee face to face,
Sheltered in Thy celestial fold,
  "A sinner saved by grace,"
What will it be Thy love to adore,
Assured I shall "go out no more?"

Rejoicing in Hope.

AND does my parting hour draw nigh,
  And is the horizon veiled in gloom,
Still I look up—and smiling say,
  "Soon, soon, the Lord will come."

Faint not, my soul! though toils and pains
  Oppress thee now (the captive's doom),
Soon thou wilt cast away thy chains,
  Soon, soon the Lord will come.

Let not my eyes with tears be dim,
  Let joy their upward glance illume;
Look up, and watch, and wait for Him—
  Soon, soon the Lord will come.

Soon will that star-paved milky way,
  Soon will that beauteous azure dome,
Glories, ne'er yet conceived, display—
  Soon, soon the Lord will come.

Changed in the twinkling of an eye,
  Invested with immortal bloom,
I shall behold Him throned on high,
  And sing, "The Lord is come!"

One beam from His all-glorious face
   These mortal garments will consume,
Each sinful blemish will efface—
   Lord Jesus, quickly come!

What will it be with Thee to dwell,
   Thyself my everlasting home!
Oh bliss—oh joy ineffable!
   Lord Jesus, quickly come!

Fear Not.

"Be not afraid! only believe,"

WHY, why art thou so fearful,
   O thou of little faith?
Why faint, desponding, tearful,
   Forgetting One who saith—
"Let not your heart be troubled,
   Nor let it be afraid;"
The charge repeated, doubled,
   Enforces what He said.

Each dark and threatening presage
  Fulfils His sacred word;
Each judgment bears His message,
  Death, pestilence, the sword:
He over all presideth,
  Withdrawn in light serene;
Each wheel minutely guideth
  Of earth's immense machine.

And still, though skies are darkening,
  His children must not fear;
To those sweet accents hearkening,
  Which whisper, "He draws near."
My soul, in Him confiding,
  Thy rock, thy hiding-place,
Beneath His wings abiding,
  Wait thou to see His face.

To herald His appearing,
  These awful signs are sent;
These storms the skies are clearing;
  Soon will the veil be rent:
Then, with His saints surrounding
  Him thou hast long adored,
Will thy sweet harp be sounding,
  "For ever with the Lord."

A Christmas Hymn.

CALM was the hallowed night!
Valley and `mountain height
   Slumbered in shade;
Roofed by heaven's azure fair,
Making their flocks their care,
Shepherds, in open air,
   Tranquilly stayed.

Suddenly round them shone,
Dazzling to look upon,
   Splendours of light;
Then drew an angel near,
And, to allay their fear,
Poured on their ravished ear
   Words of delight!

Ne'er, since the world began,
Music so sweet to man
   Sounded abroad;
On that auspicious morn,
Changing our state forlorn,
Christ as a babe was born,
   Jesus the Lord!

A Christmas Hymn.

Well might the tidings told
Waken your harps of gold,
    Chorus unseen !
Sweet rang your minstrelsy,
"Glory to God on high !"
" Peace on earth," amnesty,
    "Good will towards men !"

Well might the shepherds haste,
Ere yet the night was past,
    That thing to see ;
Where light the meteor shed
Well might the Magi tread,
Joyful, the path that led,
    Saviour, to Thee !

Infant of Bethlehem !
Now do I seek, like them,
    Thy mean abode ;
There in Thy strange disguise
Thee do I recognize,
Maker of earth and skies,
    Almighty God !

Mysteries so deep deter
Nature's proud reasoner,
    Scorning God's word :

Thee, whom the Father seals,
He to Thy seed reveals;
Each to this mandate kneels—
    "Thus saith the Lord."

"Wonderful, Counsellor!"
Thee whom the Virgin bore,
    Thee I receive;
God e'er the world began,
Perfect God, perfect man—
Mystery too deep to scan—
    This I believe.

Lo, at Thy feet I lay,
Giving myself away,
    All that is mine;
Treasures I none unfold,
Frankincense, myrrh, or gold,
One sinful heart behold,
    Take it for Thine.

Father! Thy love I bless,
Who in our deep distress
    Gavest Thy Son!
Saviour! I Thee adore,
Spirit! Thine unction pour;
Thee I praise evermore,
    Great Three in One!

Life's Evening Hour.

Sweet is life's evening hour !
    The soul looks calmly back
    O'er all the varied track,
Passed through in comfort or in pain ;
In sunshine now, and now in rain ;
    And thinks a few rough stages more
    Will land her on that peaceful shore
Where, by no weariness opprest,
She will enjoy an endless rest.

Sweet is life's evening hour !
    Its business and its toil,
    Its bustle and turmoil,
" The heat and burden of the day ;"
These have for ever passed away.
    That holy calm succeeds
    The fainting spirit needs,
Meekly, in peace, by faith and prayer,
For its last conflict to prepare.

Sweet is life's evening hour !
    What though the enfeebled frame
    Some anxious thought will claim ;

Dearer each day becomes the hope,
Firmer its ground, more wide its scope,
    That soon a wondrous change,
    More glorious e'en than strange,
This frame will suddenly transform,
And make it like the Saviour's form.

Sweet is life's evening hour!
    The Christian's steadfast eye
    Fixed on the sunset sky,
Behind those crimson clouds of gold,
Sees brighter, lovelier scenes unfold;
    Through the still air he hears
    Sounds from those upper spheres,
Which make him long to flee away,
And burst the encumbering bonds of clay!

Sweet is life's evening hour!
    The tranquil contrite breast
    In simple faith doth rest;
Grasps the salvation full and free,
Wrought out by Christ eternally
    He, in his last long sleep,
    His child will safely keep;
And when the eternal dawn shall break,
Oh! to what rapture will he wake!

To the Passing Spirit.

RANSOMED spirit! heavenward hasten!
Death's rough hand will soon unfasten
     All thy bonds of clay!
Now its radiant shores discerning,
O'er thy native country yearning,
To thy Father's house returning,
     Wing thy homeward way!

Relatives and friends immortal
Wait beyond that gloomy portal,
     Thy release to hail.
Now thy term of exile over,
Angel forms around thee hover,
Waiting till thine eye discover
     All " within the veil."

O'er thy sorrowing friends thou grievest;
God will comfort those thou leavest;
     God will be their stay!
Brief will prove their sad privation,
Glorious love's bright consummation;
There, where comes not separation,
     Spirit! haste away!

The Better Country.

Hebrews xi. 16.

OH yes! there is a land of light!
　One where the Sun no more goes down;
Wherein there shall be no more night,
　Where darkening skies no more shall frown;
And when this earth so dark appears,
Onward I look, and dry my tears.

Oh, yes, there is a land of peace!
　No jarring sound can there intrude;
There discord and contention cease;
　Those crystal walls all strife exclude!
And when earth's tumults pain my ear,
I smile and say "That land draws near."

Oh, yes, there is a land of life!
　Where glorious forms around the throne
No longer fear the dying strife—
　Suffering and death are there unknown.
When here death's ravages I see,
Oh! how I long away to flee!

Oh, yes, there is a land of love,
  Where mind with mind, and heart with heart,
Such sympathy, such oneness prove,
  As this low state can ne'er impart:
And when for love like this I yearn,
Thither my longing eyes I turn.

Oh, land of light, peace, life, and love,
  Sweet is the thought that I, ere long,
Shall to thy blissful scenes remove,
  And shine thy glorious forms among.
Saviour! I look to that bright home,
And wait and long to see Thee come.

The Twilight Hour.

THE twilight hour is come,
  The hour for musings sweet;
For breathings towards a heavenly home,
For calling back the thoughts that roam,
  Which earth's low trifles cheat:

Oh! may the Holy Spirit's power
Hallow and bless the twilight hour!

The day is past and gone!
    The sun has run his round!
All nature's course has hastened on;
Earth, sea, and sky their task have done,
    Faithful has each been found.
How has my soul pursued her track?
Have I gone forward, or gone back?

My God! throughout this day
    Thine eye has watched my heart!
Has marked each footstep of my way;
And now its penetrating ray
    Seems through my soul to dart;
Discovering the dark depths within,
And many an unsuspected sin.

What progress can I trace?
    What growth in faith and love?
What urgent cries for quickening grace?
What strenuous toil to run the race?
    What grasp of things above?
Ah! lukewarm praises, languid prayers,
Betray a heart oppressed with cares.

My loins have not been girt,
  My lamp has not been bright;
My soul, unwatchful, weak, inert,
Has failed such efforts to exert
  As draw down life and light;
No spur to others has been given,
No fragrance shed that breathes of heaven.

O Thou whose cleansing blood
  Forms my sole hope and plea,
Down to that renovating flood
Where guilt is lost and strength renewed,
  With contrite faith I flee;
Now let its healing, quickening power
Stamp value on this twilight hour.

Hymn for the New Year.

I TAKE my pilgrim staff anew,
Life's path, untrodden, to pursue,
Thy guiding eye, my Lord, I view;
    My times are in Thy hand.

Throughout the year, my heavenly Friend,
On Thy blest guidance I depend;
From its commencement to its end
    My times are in Thy hand.

Should comfort, health, and peace be mine,
Should hours of gladness on me shine,
Then let me trace Thy love divine;
    My times are in Thy hand.

But should'st Thou visit me again
With langour, sorrow, sickness, pain,
Still let this thought my hope sustain,
    My times are in Thy hand.

Thy smile alone makes moments bright,
That smile turns darkness into light;
This thought will soothe grief's saddest night,
    My times are in Thy hand.

Should those this year be called away
Who lent to life its brightest ray,
Teach me in that dark hour to say,
    My times are in Thy hand.

A few more days, a few more years,—
Oh, then a bright reverse appears,
Then I shall no more say with tears,
    My times are in Thy hand.

That hand my steps will gently guide,
To the dark brink of Jordan's tide,
Then bear me to the heavenward side ;
My times are in Thy hand.

Saturday Night.

"God requireth that which is past."—*Eccles.* iii. 15.

My fleeting days glide on with noiseless haste,
"A shadow that departeth," I go hence ;
Another week, its term of service past,
Points to its follower, waiting to commence.

Each comes in silence, leads me on my way
A little farther, then the task resigns,
They note the hours, the moments of their stay,
To Him they tell them who their post assigns.

There is a book which no erasures blot ;
A register of weeks, and days, and hours ;
He who records them faints nor wearies not,
His mind no multiplicity o'erpowers.

And when the books are opened at the last,
  That secret volume shall unfolded be;
And then the history of each moment past,
  Whilst there I stand, th' assembled world shall see.

The Wild Violet.

SWEET Spring walked forth, young flowers her path-
    way traced,
Green wreaths with silver buds adorned her hair;
The gay road-side bloomed like a garden fair,
With primroses and violets interlaced.
I plucked a handful, and with eager haste
Sought to inhale the violet's perfume rare.
Alas! the form, but not the scent, was there—
More sheltered bowers its lovelier kindred graced.
Is there no moral whispered? Are there found
None with the Christian's name, who gaily shine,
Resembling plants trained up on holy ground,
But, like this flower, who breathe no scent divine?
Not on the world's broad road can grow such flowers
As Piety trains up in her blest bowers.

99

Prayer to the Holy Spirit.

Holy Spirit! mighty God!
Send Thy glorious light abroad,
Through each chamber of my soul,
Bending all to Thy control;
All renewing, all transforming,
My whole mind to Christ's conforming:
What He values let me prize;
Let me all things else despise.

What did He of value deem?
Did He this world's joys esteem?
Wealth or grandeur, rank or fame,
Did He seek them, or disclaim?
Poor, despised, of humble birth,
Having not a home on earth;
Gold or silver He had none,
Called not aught on earth His own.

Satan's empire to destroy
Was His object and His joy;
Heal the miseries caused by sin,
For His Father souls to win;

To the contrite peace to impart,
Binding up the broken heart;
Pouring light upon the mind,
Vision on the inly blind.

Thus His mission to fulfil,
Thus to do His Father's will,
Was the only joy He sought;
Night and day for this He wrought.
Sowing seed each day with care,
Watering it each night with prayer;
And with Godlike love and power
Scattering blessings every hour.

Wondrous was the race He ran,
Marvellous His love to man!
Meek and lowly, though so great,
Washing His disciples' feet :
He, the holiest, did descend
To be called the "sinner's Friend;"
And to shame all human pride,
"Numbered with transgressors" died.

Blessed Spirit! by Thee led,
In His footsteps let me tread;
Seek the objects that He sought,
Labour for the souls He bought;

Pleasing not myself, but still
Doing all my Father's will;
Growing more and more in love,
Till I see His face above.

A Winter Sunset.

DARK clouds hung brooding o'er the cold grey sea,
And wintry blasts all mournfully swept by,
But in th' horizon, towards the western sky,
One spot like burnished gold appeared to be;
An emblem glad, and beautiful to see:
For there the wave met day's refulgent eye,
And not one envious shadow lingered nigh,
Where poured his stream of splendour, full and free.
Christian ! this typifies thy life's dark stream,
Throughout its course o'erhung with many a cloud;
While brief and fitful is the golden gleam,
That tells how bright a sun those vapours shroud;
But when the wave reflects the setting ray,
A flood of glory melts each cloud away.

The Universal Hymn.

TRAVELLER on earth ! mark well its fabric rare,
   So passing fair !
Survey its leafy aisles, its towering dome ;
   Let thine eye roam
O'er all the beauteous colours there inlaid,
The star-embroidered tracery displayed.

Then listen to its choir—their matin song
   So sweet, yet strong !
And when the sun declines and day grows dim,
   Their vesper hymn !
While soft responses woods and waters make,
As gentle winds their sweet low voices wake.

Nor wants there fragrant incense, heavenward borne
   Both night and morn,
From dew-decked flowers, earth's habitants unstained,
   Who pure remained
When fell that blight the *moral* garden shares ;
Of Eden telling, each his censer bears.

103

Christian ! the priest of this ethereal fane
Mark not in vain
Its fair proportions, its melodious choir !
The altar's fire
Thy sacrifice must call for ; lowly bend,
Offer thy heart, then will the flame descend.

Watchers unseen, from the upper Temple sent,
Listening attent,
Stand mid the leafy arches, till *thou* grace
The foremost place,
And lead the choirs, and make its songs to be
An echo of its own sweet minstrelsy.

New Year's Eve.

I SATE in silence listening
To the retreating year;
I heard its latest hour take wing—
A shrouded Form stood near,
Pointing to time's fast narrowing shore,
And whispering "Soon 'twill be no more."

I felt alone and desolate,
   And all looked dark around;
My thoughts were like a heavy weight,
   Which on my heart seemed bound :
I mused on life's ephemeral span,
And sighed "O miserable man !"

The past, in mournful retrospect,
   Awoke my griefs and fears;
The present no fair colours decked ;
   I viewed it through my tears :
Sickness and sorrow, pain and death,
All closed me round and choked my breath.

But then, though faintly, fearfully,
   I sought the throne of grace;
Full oft had light and hope for me
   Beamed from that hallowed place;
My heavy load of thought and care,
My sins, my griefs, I took them there.

Oh blessed, blessed antidote
   For every mental woe !
Which hushes each distracting thought
   The human heart can know!
At once a heavenly light stole o'er
That scene so dark, so sad before !

That ocean, dark and shadowy,
   On which I feared to gaze,
Soon, like a golden sunset sea,
   Shone with a thousand rays;
And One appeared its waves to span,
"Whose form was like the Son of Man."

He spoke with voice so musical,
   As quite entranced the ear;
"Thy sins," He said, "I bore them all—
   They cannot reappear;
And earth is clouded o'er for thee,
That thou may'st long to be with Me."

The Name above every Name.

"The name of the Lord is a strong tower."

Thou, through whose all-prevailing name
I urge my every plea and claim,
   The Holy One, the Just!
Jesus! Thy name's mysterious power
Shall guard me through life's dangerous hour,
   And be in death my trust.

Oh, precious name! my tower of strength,
My resting-place, through all the length
    And toil of life's rough way;
When vexed with cares, oppressed with woes,
Still, still *in Thee* I find repose,
    On Thee my soul I stay.

Thou brightest, dearest, holiest name
Of Him unchangeably the same,
    My Hope, my Shield, my All!
Be Thou my song, my theme, my boast,
Till, with His countless ransomed host,
    Low at His feet I fall.

Thou art the burden of heaven's song,
The theme of all the saintly throng
    Enthroned in realms of light;
To Thee each golden harp is strung,
Thy praise by each sweet voice is sung,
    With ever new delight.

Name above every name be Thou,
That to which every knee shall bow,
    Each human heart shall bless!
Jehovah! Jesus! tune each voice
In Thee, Thee only, to rejoice,
    " The Lord our Righteousness."

Look Upward.

" I will lift up mine eyes unto the hills, from whence cometh my help."—*Ps.* cxxi. 1.

WHEN earth's supports and comforts fail,
When shadows lengthen o'er the vale,
When those who loved us fall asleep,
And leave us still to watch and weep;
Then grasp the hope so freely given,
Then turn from earth and look to heaven!

When still where'er the eye is cast
It meets a lone and dreary waste,
And, stripped of all its Summer leaves,
Life's wilderness thy spirit grieves;
Then to Faith's eye new worlds are given:
Oh turn from earth and look to heaven!

His hand whose guidance cannot err,
Thy Father, Saviour, Comforter,
He, whom thine heartfelt praises bless,
Guides, guards thee through the wilderness:
And hourly cordials shall be given,
Till earth shall be exchanged for heaven!   •

The Holy Comforter!

HOLY Comforter! my Guide!
Now within my heart abide;
Nothing do I need beside;
   Fill my soul with light.

Each celestial truth reveal;
Christ's rich treasury unseal;
Thine indwelling let me feel,
   Fount of pure delight!

While a little longer space
Here my lonely path I trace,
Pour within rich streams of grace;
   Form a garden there.

Then, though all around may be
But a wilderness for me,
Sheltered from its dearth by Thee,
   All things will seem fair.

While Thou deign'st my heart to bless
With Thy presence, Thy sweet peace,
Can I pine in loneliness?
   Can I wish for more?

No! Thou Comforter Divine,
If Thy fellowship be mine,
Earthly converse I resign,
     Fondly prized before.

Life was for this end bestowed,
To acquaint myself with God:
Oft the loneliest pathway trod
     Nearer leads to Him.

Guide into all truth! be Thou
My Divine Instructor now;
Be my views no longer low,
     Indistinct and dim!

Rend the darkening veil that shrouds
Those bright scenes above the clouds;
Show me those serene abodes
     Where "is no more night."

Where the Father and the Son,
With Thyself for ever one,
Shed from the eternal throne
     Everlasting light.

Then will all the shadows here
Lose their charms, and disappear,
Lost in that resplendent sphere
     Opened to Faith's eye.

Quickened by its glorious ray
I shall hasten on my way,
Till I drop these bonds of clay
And to Jesus fly.

The New Jerusalem.

JERUSALEM, blest city of our God!
How oft the pilgrim's thoughts on thee repose,
While turning from life's conflicts, toils, and woes,
He looks afar to thy serene abode!
Then, strengthened and refreshed, pursues his road,
While Faith exults and Hope with ardour glows;
Joyful he hastens on, for soon he knows
Abundant entrance will be there bestowed!
He mourns not that his intervals of rest
Are here so short, so broken, and so few;
Nor yet, that when he fain would build his nest,
A hand unseen yet "stirs it up" anew;
"Jerusalem," he cries, "while here I roam,
Be thou my spirit's rest, her only home."

Sunday Morning.

Sabbath of rest, all hail!
Sweet pause from earthly care!
When the glad soul expands her wings,
Forgets terrestrial thoughts and things,
And breathes a purer air;
Attunes her lyre
To that blest choir
She hopes ere long to join, whose themes her notes
inspire.

Sabbath of rest, all hail!
Fair type of future bliss!
Who comest like an angel sent
To charm each week of banishment,
Passed in a world like this;
To urge the soul
To reach the goal,
Where glory's fadeless wreath will all her griefs
console.

Sabbath of rest, all hail!
Day of discourse divine!
When He who once to Emmaus walked
With those who thought on Him, and talked,
Draws near with love benign;
To Faith's clear eye,
Seems very nigh;
His glory deigns to unveil—His word to ratify.

Sabbath of rest, all hail!
Come thou, and set me free
From earth's entanglements and cares,
From sin's deceits, from Satan's snares!
Let every sound
I breathe around,
With heaven's own choral song in unison be found.

Lord of the Sabbath! Thou
Whose smile all joy inspires;
Disclose the brightness of Thy face!
Reveal the riches of Thy grace!
Fill all my soul's desires:
Her quickened ear,
With filial fear,
Words of eternal life now waits from Thee to hear.

The Man of Sorrows.

Dost thou complain of sorrow? Look on Him!
His visage marred, His eye with suffering dim;
The load of unknown agony He bore
Forced out great drops of blood from every pore.
Sharest thou His sorrows? Oh! how small a part!
For God's rebuke did even break His heart.

Dost thou complain of want? Thy Lord, thy Head,
Was meanly lodged, was coarsely clothed and fed:
He hungered and was thirsty; faint with heat;
He walked from place to place with weary feet;
What couch of rest was His who came to save?
A manger, first,—a cross,—and then a grave.

Dost thou complain of coldness, slighting, scorn?
Look on thy Lord, deserted and forlorn!
Who had such right devoted love to expect,
Yet met with such unparalleled neglect?
E'en in His bitterest grief no friend was given,
Denied alike all help from earth and heaven.

The Man of Sorrows.

Dost thou complain of shame and deep disgrace?
Look on thy sinless Lord, and hide thy face!
Stripped, crowned with thorns, scourged, spit on, set
To trial as a malefactor brought,—   [at naught,
Then crucified with thieves, in public view,
The death of vilest criminals the due.

Dost thou complain of that worst evil, sin,—
And mourn its deep defilement spread within?
Lay thy sick soul beneath that cross one hour,
The deadly venom loses there its power—
A stream flows thence which, though of crimson glow,
Makes the polluted soul as white as snow.

Dost thou complain of agonizing pain?
Behold that cross! Behold it not in vain!
View those racked limbs, that torn and bleeding brow,
Hark! from that tortured Form what accents flow!
Prayer for His murderers' pardon! words of balm,
His mother's anguish to console and calm!

Dost thou complain because thou soon must die?
Look on thy Lord, nor dread the parting sigh!
He drank the bitterest potion death ere gave,
And to a bed of rest transformed the grave :—
In death, in life, in want, pain, guilt or grief,
Look to that cross, there seek and find relief.

Weep Not.

" Blessed are the dead which die in the Lord."

MOURN not for those who die !
If suffering nature, sad and weak,
  Must shed the tear and heave the sigh,
Wouldst thou the well of comfort seek ?
  Mourner ! thy lost ones live on high !
The Father has but called His own ;
Bend thee, and say, "Thy will be done !"
  Mourn not for them !

Mourn not ! they are not dead !
No, they have burst the galling chain
  That bound them to this dungeon world ;
Their souls with their Redeemer reign,
  Love's banner o'er them floats unfurled !
For ever and for ever blest
Are they who in their Saviour rest ;
  Mourn not for them !

Mourn not ! they live for aye !
Death's stingless shafts in vain are cast,
  And vainly yawns the grave's deep gloom ;
The tyrant's shadowy reign is past,

Burst the dark barriers of the tomb !
Sin dies in death ! all sorrow dies !
To endless bliss the ransomed rise !
Rejoice for them !

The Scriptures.

THERE is a wondrous volume, on whose page
Shines heavenly truth in characters of light,
For ever lasting and for ever bright,
Immutably the same from age to age ;
Its light is life. Philosopher and sage
Dwell on its charms with reverence and delight,
When from earth's film their intellectual sight
The Spirit deigns to cleanse and disengage.
All other volumes lose their zest and tire ;
But this, the more its treasures we unfold,
Exceeding far the costliest gems or gold,
Fill to the utmost all the soul's desire :
Wisdom to guide, and balm to heal, supplies ;
Enlightens, comforts, cheers, and satisfies.

To a Friend setting out on a Journey.

MAY heavenly guides attend thee !
May heavenly guards defend thee !
May heavenly influence send thee
    Sweet themes for holy thought !
Though shades of night enfold thee,
That Eye will still behold thee,
    E'en His who slumbers not !

No evil shall befal thee,
No enemy appal thee,
Bright messengers shall call thee,
    Throughout the silent night,
To share their high communion,
Sweet pledge of future union
    With sainted heirs of light.

No human voice may cheer thee,
No earthly listener hear thee,
But oh ! one Friend is near thee,
    The kindest and the best !
Whose smile can banish sadness,
Whose presence fills with gladness
    The solitary breast.

Thy God will go before thee,
And day and night watch o'er thee,
And safely soon restore thee
    To thy loved home in peace;
Nor will His care diminish
Till life's long journey finish,
    And toils and dangers cease.

Easter Eve.

HOLY Slumberer, rest in peace!
Now Thy toils and conflicts cease;
Now the glorious victory won,
Death and Satan overthrown,
Soon will burst the exulting strain,
"Worthy is the Lamb once slain!"

We are watching round Thy tomb;
Angel wings flit through the gloom,
And the blissful morn draws nigh
When, through earth, and air, and sky,
Shall the wondrous news be spread—
"Christ is risen from the dead!"

Happy those who saw Thee then;
"Fairer than the sons of men;"
Happy those to whom 'twas given
To behold Thee rise to heaven!
We a blessing, too, receive,
"Who, not having seen, believe."

Saviour of once ruined man!
Sealed is the stupendous plan:
On its bright, triumphant close
Firmly all our hopes repose.
Oh! to feel each day, each hour,
More Thy resurrection's power.

Hallowed Sleep.

OH, what a tranquil, hallowed sleep
Is theirs whom Christ doth safely keep!
    Whose dust His angels guard!
Oh, what a waking will be theirs
When all the glories He prepares
    Shall be their bright reward!

They will awake in beauty clad,
In immortality arrayed;
    Strength that can ne'er decay;
Awake to such a life of bliss
As, in a troubled world like this,
    Fancy can scarce pourtray.

Awake to be for ever freed
From all those barriers that impede
    Our growth and progress here;
Freed from that heaviest weight of all,
Sin's taint, transmitted from the fall,
    Its power no more to fear.

But more, far more they will awake
Their Saviour's likeness to partake,
    His presence to adore;
His voice to hear, His smile to meet,
His praise unwearied to repeat,
    When time shall be no more.

Who then shall fear to fall asleep,
Who for those happy spirits weep
    Who now in Christ are blest?
Ah, rather let us long and pray,
And haste towards that blessed day,
    When we shall share their rest.

My Home.

" I go to prepare a place for you."

"My home, my home, my happy home!"
　　Yes! there is music in the words—
And the sweet sound, while here I roam,
　　Thrills my rapt spirit's deepest chords :—
Thither, full oft, I lift my eye,—
My happy home, for thee I sigh!

"My home, my home, my happy home!"
　　Can I the phrase too oft repeat?
'Midst scenes which sin has tinged with gloom,
　　Traversed in pain, with weary feet!
Oh no, to heaven I lift my eye,
"My home, my happy home!" I cry.

"My home, my home, my happy home!"
　　How many loved ones, there at rest,
Wait for the blissful hour to come,
　　When the desires which fill my breast,
All, all shall consummated be,
My home, my happy home, in thee!

"My home, my home, my happy home!"
   Dwells He not there whom most I love?
My country lies beyond the tomb;
   My heart is given to one above:
Oh death, I even long, through thee,
My home, my happy home to see.

For the First Sunday of a New Year.

WELCOME, sweet day of holy peace!
   When earth a hallowed spot appears;
Its toils and cares and tumults cease,
   And heavenly sounds delight our ears.

Welcome, sweet day of bounteous grace!
   When from their unseen sources flow
Streams which refresh this desert place,
   And bid the flowers of Eden blow.

Welcome, sweet day of boundless love!
   When, as man communes with his friends,
The God of glory from above
   His saints to visit condescends.

123

Welcome sweet day of faith divine!
  When on the precious "Corner Stone,"
Simply recumbent, they recline,
  Fixed and built up on Him alone.

Welcome, sweet day of joyful hope!
  When the winged soul from bondage freed,
Can give her boundless wishes scope,
  And on celestial banquets feed.

Welcome sweet day of heart-felt praise!
  When, mingling with immortal choirs,
We blend with theirs our grateful lays,
  To Him whose love their harps inspires.

Welcome, sweet day of fervent prayers!
  When our High Priest His word fulfils;
Our names upon His breastplate bears,
  For us His golden censer fills.

Thrice welcome, day of converse sweet!
  For those whose hearts breathe love to Him;
While all His goodness they repeat,
  Bright glows the flame earth's vapours dim.

Sweet Sabbath! first-fruits of the year!
  Its opening bud, its dawning ray!
Be thou its type, its emblem dear;
  Be its whole course one Sabbath day!

The Search for Happiness.

" Her ways are ways of pleasantness, and all her paths are peace."
Prov. iii. 17.

WHERE is happiness, oh where?
Breathes she not the mountain air,
Where the wild thyme scents the breeze,
And enchanting prospects please?
  No, oh no !
  Bending low,
In a tranquil spot withdrawn,
Greeting thus the golden dawn ;
There I caught her radiant smile,
There she tarried for awhile.

Treads she not the classic halls,
Where the light of science falls
On the lore of years gone by,
Solving truth's deep mystery?
  No, oh no !
  Whispering low
In a chamber small but neat,
Soothing pain with comfort sweet ;
There I caught her radiant smile,
There she tarried for awhile.

Seeks she not the banquet bright,
Splendid rooms lit up at night;
Gay with mirth and music sweet,
And the merry dancers' feet?
    No, oh no!
    Soft and slow
Reading words of truth divine,
Pondering o'er each sacred line;
There I caught her radiant smile,
There she tarried for awhile.

Seeks she ne'er the crowded mart,
There to take a busy part
In the schemes of high emprise,
Which to fame and affluence rise?
    No, oh no!
    Here below
She but seeks one jewel rare,
One rich pearl absorbs her care;
When she finds it, mark her smile!
Heaven seems opening the while!

Shuns she, then, the joys of earth?
Dreads she cheerfulness and mirth?
She is called "a serious thing;"
Glooms and shadows does she bring?

126

No, oh no !
Brightly glow
On her garments, on her brow,
Lovelier hues than earth can show;
But from heaven is caught her smile,
Here she visits for awhile.

The Way, the Truth, and the Life.

I CANNOT wander far astray,
For Thou, my Saviour, art " the Way ;"
I know no perfect way beside,
I know but one unerring guide.

My soul, while this blest path I tread,
By no false lights will be misled ;
Thy doctrines satisfy the heart—
My God, " the Truth " itself Thou art.

That heart Thou deignest now to share,
Thou'rt formed " the hope of glory " there ;
Soon I shall quit this world of strife,
And feel in death Thou art " the Life."

To a Mourner.

A VOICE beloved thus spoke of late
In sad yet chastened tone—
"My heart at times *is* desolate.
　　　　"I feel alone."

I looked upon that loved one's brow,
And read the traces there
Those who have suffered learn to know
　　　　Of grief and care.

Though now the storms have passed away,
Enough remains to mark
That life has been a wintry day,
　　　　Stormy and dark.

So stands some tempest-riven tree,
Its fairest branches gone;
It ne'er what once it was can be
　　　　Ere storms came down.

Yet, mourner, though tears filled my eye,
And dimmed my thoughtful gaze,
I looked on thee rejoicingly,
　　　　And gave God praise.

What though thine earthly hopes are crushed,
Thine earthly wishes crossed,
Those voices sweet in silence hushed
        That cheered thee most:

Does not a voice more cheering still
New hopes, new joys impart?
And thoughts of holiest power instil,
        To heal thy heart?

Hast thou not meekly learned to bow,
With acquiescing love,
To Him whose hand has brought thee low,
        His love to prove?

Does not thy faith strike deeper roots?
Blest who that faith possess!
Are there not formed the peaceful fruits
        Of righteousness?

Oh, yes! the process I behold,
And joyfully admire,
Through which thou wilt come forth as gold
        Tried in the fire.

Concealed from man the dross may lie,
Now with the metal mixed;
But on it the Refiner's eye
        Is calmly fixed.

Nor will He leave (this thought is joy)
The gold He thus refines,
Till in it, pure from all alloy,
      His image shines.

On a Departed Friend.

Yes, she was very lovely; soft, serene;
A heavenly impress rested on her brow;
Methinks I view her sweet pale features now,
As on her sister's arm she loved to lean;
While in her whole demeanour there were seen
Meek resignation, love's seraphic glow,
And faith, which, when earth's hopes were all laid low,
Could look, rejoicing, to a happier scene.
Blessed is thy sweet memory, much-loved saint,
Precious to all who shared thy converse here;
As the pure gold, when purged from dross and taint,
Shows the Refiner's likeness, mirror'd clear,
So, from the furnace coming forth, in thee,
'Twas ours thy Lord's reflected traits to see.

Let me go; for the Day breaketh.

LET me go : for the day now breaketh,
Let me go where the heart ne'er acheth,—
Where not one the cup of woe partaketh,
    But the weary are at rest.
Let me go where the strength ne'er faileth,
Where the blighting curse no more prevaileth,
Where the serpent's sting no more assaileth,
    Where nor foe nor fear molest.

Let me go : for my spirit fainteth
To dwell in that world no evil tainteth,
To look on the vision no pencil painteth,
    Which no mortal eye hath seen.
Let me go : for my heart is weary,
Around me the wintry gloom is dreary,
But the summer in heaven is bright and cheery,
    And the deep blue sky serene.

Let me go : for the best and dearest,
The treasures who once to my heart were nearest,—
Whose love was the fondest, best, sincerest,
    They are all gone before.

I feel upon earth a lonely stranger,
Compassed with sorrow and care and danger,
Amid wastes and wilds a trembling ranger:
    Let me go to a fairer shore.

Let me go. The glad word is spoken—
The golden bowl at the fount is broken;
Loosed is the silver cord, in token
    That my task is done below.
Let me go—to the God who sought me,
To the Saviour whose precious blood hath bought me,
To the heavenly Guide who hath cleansed and
      taught me,
    Oh, let me, let me go!

On Sacred Music.

It is said that the exile who chances to hear
   In the land of the stranger his own native tongue,
Or some strain that in childhood delighted his ear,
   Though he listen with rapture, yet weeps o'er the
      song.

For then what bright visions appear to his view !
  What scenes of enchantment rise quickly around !
The land where the first breath of freedom he drew,
  His home, his loved kindred, he seems to have
    found !

But though sweet the delusion, not long can it last :
  In a moment the lovely deceptions are flown :
With the sounds that produced them too quickly
    they passed,
  And the exile still finds himself sad and alone.

And is not the Christian an exile on earth?
  And is not sweet music the language of heaven,
Of that land whence the spirit received her high birth,
  And from whence the bright grant of her freedom
    was given?

And thus, while he listens to anthems of praise,
  Or some soft-stealing melody falls on his ear,
Those regions of joy he in spirit surveys,
  And seems the sweet song of the ransomed to
    hear.

Nay, he seems to have entered that haven of rest,
  To have bidden farewell to temptations and woes ;
Already he joins the bright bands of the blest,
  Already partakes their eternal repose.

But the charm is soon broken ; the sounds die away ;
  No mandate, as yet, is sent down of release :
He mourns to perceive still so distant the day,
  When his suff'rings and labours for ever shall
    cease.

That day of delight, when, an exile no more,
  His country, his home, his loved friends he regains,
Tunes his harp to the chorus oft longed for before,
  Where "sorrow and sighing" ne'er blend with the
    strains.

A Simile.

ONCE on a cloudy, wintry day
I marked a beauteous golden ray
On the waves' rippling surface play,
    As swift it glided on ;
The cold grey water changed its hue ;
O'er it the sun his mantle threw ;
Its gentle course more radiant grew,
    A track of light it shone.

Sun of my soul! my life would be
Like that cold wave, untouched by Thee!
Thus shine 'midst wintry gloom on me,
  Thus make my darkness light;
Moving with calm yet lustrous force,
Though winds and storms swell wild and hoarse,
Make Thou my onward, heaven-lit course
  Still to the end more bright!

Stanzas for a Friend in Sorrow.

It must be so; the feeling heart must oft receive
 a wound;
Must often be compelled to part from those it
 twined around:
It must be so; life's shadows still must lengthen
 o'er our way,
And darkness those bright places fill, where shone
 joy's sunniest ray.

It must be so; the hopes of youth, the schemes
 gay fancy wove,   [prove;
The fictions we believed as truth, must all delusive

And e'en in manhood's riper day, with wisdom for
    our guide,
The prop selected for our stay oft proves a reed
    when tried.

It must be so; our hours of bliss, like a sweet
    April gleam,
Just smile on such a world as this, then vanish like
    a dream;
Hope's Iris, with its beauteous braid, melts in the
    clouds it wreathes;
Joy's roseate flower begins to fade, e'en while its
    fragrance breathes.

It must be so; the friends beloved, who cheered
    life's earlier day,
By time estranged, by death removed, pass one by
    one away;
Till oft, ere half its sands can fall, we look around
    and sigh—
" How many now my tears recall whose smile once
    blest my eyes!"

While o'er the heart these changes come, and man,
    earth's transient guest,
Learns that the soul has here no home, no seat of
    tranquil rest;

'Then whither turns that eye, now dim with disap-
pointed hope?
Asks he fair Truth to draw for him her heavenly
horoscope?

Alas! too oft he turns to Grief; calls back enjoyments past,
Lives o'er again those moments brief, too blest, too
bright to last;
Forgets that bitters marred the sweet, and thorns
the flowers, e'en then;
Feels that his sun of bliss has set, and twilight days
remain.

Or if from Grief he pass away, to seek a sterner
guide,
Philosophy! he courts thy sway, thy loftier code is
tried:
But Reason the firm mind may win, and nerve its
high resolves,
While on its axis, dark within, the restless heart
revolves.

'Tis braced and disciplined, not healed; its wounds
are stanched, not cured;
These moral anodynes but yield calm midst the
pain endured:

Not this the kind result designed by Him who,
    from above,
Thus breaks each tie too strongly twined, that we
    may seek His love.

E'en as the bird "stirs up her nest," to make her
    nurslings fly,
He here forbids us to find rest, towards heaven to
    raise our eye:
The sunshine is from earth removed, that heaven
    more bright may seem,
The heart denied what most it loved, till there He
    reign supreme.

Then all around a light is shed, which ne'er will
    fade away;
More radiant grows the path we tread, e'en "to the
    perfect day;"
Each wound is healed, each want supplied, joys
    given which leave us never;
The heart's deep longing satisfied, and satisfied for
    ever!

On an Early Violet

SCARCELY has one bright sunbeam shone,
  Or vernal zephyr waved its wing;
Yet is thy fragrance round me thrown,
    Sweet child of spring!

'Mid leafless shrubs, on the cold earth,
  Rises thy soft and beauteous form,
Familiar, even from thy birth,
    With many a storm.

There, blooming in thy lonely bed,
  Enfolded in thy mantle green.
Thy solitary sweets were shed,
    Unknown, unseen.

Yet, could the balmiest breath of May
  To thee one added charm have lent?
Could brighter tints thy leaves inlay,
    Or sweeter scent?

'Tis often thus; the richest flowers
  That in the soul's fair garden blow,
Are nurtured by rough winds and showers,
    'Mid scenes of woe.

When earthly joys lie all entombed,
 And life looks desolate and drear,
Then first hope's heavenly flower has bloomed,
  The heart to cheer.

Nay, thus in Sorrow's wintry day
 The soul herself, 'mid blast and storm,
Gains beauties which joy's summer ray
  Will rarely form.

Nor shall one blast around her blow,
 One storm on her fair blossoms beat,
But shall a lovelier hue bestow,
  A scent more sweet.

Summer Evening by the Seaside.

RADIANT and fair smiled ocean, sky, and strand;
Only to live, and gaze on them, seemed bliss!
The rippling silver waves stole on to kiss,
As if in sport, the smooth and glittering sand;
Soft blew the southern breezes, freshening bland;
While in the west, sheeting with gold th' abyss,

To the Nightingale.

The sunset showed a lovelier world than this,
And tipt each sail, like skiffs from fairy land.
A fulness of delight my soul o'erpowered—
And, while with thrilling ectasy I gazed,
Methought, if o'er this earth such charms are
      showered,
Oh to what heights of rapture will be raised
Each spirit destined for that pure abode,
Where, throned in glory, dwells the triune God!

To the Nightingale.

SWEET chantress! from every blossoming tree
There is wafted a song of rejoicing and glee;
Midst the mirth and the music I listen for thee,
    But thy melody charms not my ear.
When the sun shall descend, and the blossoms all
    close,
When darkness and stillness shall usher repose,
Oh then, while the night-breeze refreshingly blows,
    Thy song from afar I shall hear.

Sweet chantress! a beautiful emblem thou art,
Of the pure and devoted and tranquillized heart,
When, from early turmoil and intrusion apart,
    It holds converse with regions above;
Beneath that blue concave, so peaceful and bright,
Sweet symphonies break on the silence of night;
While angels bend down, with approving delight,
    Taking part in the anthems they love.

The Hour of Prayer.

My God! is any hour so sweet,
   From blush of morn to evening-star,
As that which calls me to Thy feet,—
      The hour of prayer?

Blest is that tranquil hour of morn,
   And blest that hour of solemn eve,
When on the wings of prayer up-borne,
      The world I leave!

For then a day-spring shines on me,
  Brighter than morn's ethereal glow;
And richer dews descend from Thee
          Than earth can know.

Then is my strength by Thee renewed;
  Then are my sins by Thee forgiven;
Then dost Thou cheer my solitude
          With hope of heaven.

No words can tell what sweet relief
  There for my every want I find,
What strength for warfare, balm for grief,
          What peace of mind.

Hushed is each doubt; gone every fear,
  My spirit seems in heaven to stay:
And e'en the penitential tear
          Is wiped away.

Lord! till I reach yon blissful shore,
  No privilege so dear shall be,
As thus my inmost soul to pour
          In prayer to thee.

The Lord turned, and looked upon Peter.

St. Luke xxii. 61.

Oh ! it is ever thus. That Eye benign
Beams on the soul with tenderness divine,
E'en ere the wanderer owns that he has strayed,
E'en ere the penitent has wept or prayed;
And when that look, that pitying look is felt,
The softened heart in contrite grief will melt,
Mourn that against such goodness it has striven,
And "love Him much" who has so "much for
    given."
The Saviour changes not, but now sends down,
E'en from His glorious mediatorial throne,
Whence all our wandering footsteps He can trace,
The same sweet tokens of forgiving grace.
Oh ! let the trembling and desponding mind,
That "broken spirit" which He loves to bind,
Dwell on each proof of tenderness He gave,
Nor doubt His willingness to heal and save!
Not e'en the fondest love a mother knows,—
The warmest in a human breast which glows,—
No loftiest, best conception we can raise,
E'en the faint outline of His love portrays.

Poor, doubting mourner! yield not to thy fears;
Each tear He numbers, and each sigh He hears;
And though, like Peter, thou hast wronged thy Lord,
Like him, thou mayest be pardoned and restored.
For thee thy Saviour's prayer may yet prevail;
True faith in Him, though weak, shall never fail;
But lead thee, in His strength, henceforth to prove,
Through life, in death, thy gratitude and love.

The Young Believer's Prayer.

" Seek ye the Lord while He may be found, call ye upon Him
while He is near." —*Isa.* lv. 6.

O God! may I look up to Thee?
  I would address Thee if I may;
And this my one request should be,
    Teach me to pray.

Now, in my sorrow, I would ask,
  What thoughts to think, what words to say;
Prayer is a new and arduous task;
    Teach me to pray.

A heartless form will not suffice,
  The self-deemed rich are sent away;
The heart must bring the sacrifice—
    Teach me to pray.

To whom shall I, Thy creature, turn?
  Whom else address? whom else obey?
Teach me the lesson I would learn—
    Teach me to pray.

Now, in my hour of trouble, deign
  To bow my spirit to Thy sway;
Now, let me ask Thee not in vain—
    Teach me to pray.

To Thee alone my eyes look up,
  Turn not, O God, Thy face away,
Prayer is my only door of hope—
    Teach me to pray.

On a Spring Morning.

Thou! who art ever present, though unseen,
Amid these beauteous shades I feel Thee near:
I seem to stand beside Thee, and to hear
That voice which makes the troubled heart serene.

I love to think Thou on this earth hast been,
And once in human form didst sojourn here,
Where still Thou deign'st invisibly to cheer
Each fainting spirit that on Thee would lean.
Oh! while in hill and dale, and stream and flower,
With tearful joy Thy glories I behold,
On me display Thy wonder-working power!
Bid each long-dormant heavenly seed unfold;
And while around woods, hills, and valleys sing,
Within my heart wake a celestial spring!

The Sure Guide.

"And Jacob awaked out of his sleep, and said, Surely the Lord is in this place, and I knew it not!"—*Gen.* xxviii. 16.

Am I to this seclusion brought,
As wandering Jacob first was taught,
  In solitude and woe,
To look on things before unseen,
And, in the stilly night serene,
  His Father's God to know?

As alone and weary he was laid,
A wondrous ladder was displayed,
  Reaching from earth to heaven ;
Ascending and descending there,
Angels (who perhaps made him their care)
  To his charmed sight were given.

He felt that God was in that place,
He learned to prize and seek His grace,
  And there before Him vowed—
"That if, through all his future track,
"He thither came, in safety back,
  "The Lord should be his God."

Like him, a wanderer I have been,
And waking, in this lonely scene,
  I feel that God is here ;
While, bright with supernatural ray,
Shines forth that " new and living way "
  Which brings the sinner near.

Apart from man, in this still hour,
He, who might crush me by His power,
  A covenant deigns to make ;
And if, supplying all my need,
He, to the end, my steps will lead,
  Him for my God I take.

If health once more He deign to give,
Then for His glory may I live,
　　May all to Him be given!
If not, while angels o'er me bend,
Those golden steps may I ascend
　　Which lead the soul to heaven!

Sonnet to the Harp.

Poor tuneless harp! I take thee to my Lord;
Though all unmeet to offer at His shrine,
If He endue my hand with skill divine,
Sweet melody shall breathe from every chord;
And thou to that high use shall be restored
Which erst in sinless paradise was thine:
I lay thee at His feet, no longer mine;
The strings all mute till wakened at His word.
Oh! thou wert formed in those unsullied days
When joy, love, innocence, attuned each lyre,
To blend thy music with celestial lays;
And e'en my notes shall mingle with that choir,
If He, th' eternal soul of harmony,
Now, by His Spirit, deign to breathe on me.

Prayer for Faith.

"Christ shall give thee light."—*Eph.* v. 14.

LORD of all power and might !
Grant me that inward sight
  Which views the things unseen ;
All earthly objects fade,
My life a fleeting shade,
Ne'er for one moment stayed,
  Will soon have crossed the scene.

Each moment it moves on,
Still hastening to be gone,
  Till, seen on earth no more,
I reach that unknown state
Where souls Thy sentence wait,
To fix their lasting fate,
  And hope of change is o'er.

Now, while there yet is time,
While earth's brief day grows dim—
  Darkened by pain and woe ;
Kindle that lamp of faith
Which can make bright my path,
E'en through the vale of death,
  If thither now I go.

Man cannot wake the spark
In my soul's chamber dark—
　Nor keep the flame alive;
Kindling Thyself the light,
Deign Thou to keep it bright,
Till, where is no more night,
　In safety I arrive.

Thoughts in Seclusion.

"In the day of adversity consider."—*Eccles.* vii. 14.

LORD, by Thy hand withdrawn apart
　From earthly things and outward scenes;
What lessons wouldst Thou teach my heart?
　What barrier break that intervenes?

Perchance to man my life has seemed
　Blameless, defiled by no dark blot;
But blameless can that life be deemed
　In which my God has been forgot?

151

Is it Thy wanderer to reclaim,
  That thou contendest now with me?
Have I not missed life's noblest aim
  As yet, not having lived for Thee?

How have my powers been misapplied!
  How has a creature, born to die,
Been borne along the impetuous tide
  Of worldly care and vanity!

Truths heard of by the outward ear
  I now discern, at least in part;
" A still small voice " I seem to hear,
  Speaking in mercy to my heart.

I boast of innocence no more;
  Guilty, yea guilty, Lord, I plead;
My merits, trusted in before,
  Now fail me like a broken reed.

Hard is that heart which ne'er has felt
  The love of God to sinful man;
Which has not learned to mourn and melt,
  Pondering salvation's wondrous plan.

" Blest is the man Thou chastenest, Lord!"
  Thus speaks the oracle divine;
Now, on my heart let grace be poured,
  And may that blessedness be mine!

To an Aged Christian on his Birthday.

Now, pilgrim! of thy journey home
 But one short, stage remains;
And, brightening through the evening's gloom,
 Across the distant plains

Methinks thine eye may catch a sight
 Of that sweet shore of rest
Where friends are waiting, robed in white,
 To hail the expected guest;

Where every hope, yet incomplete,
 Each unfulfilled desire,
Fruition's plenitude shall meet,
 Till bliss can rise no higher.

O! did our hearts indeed receive
 Faith in her power sublime,
The Christian would rejoice, not grieve,
 To mark the lapse of time.

Nature may weep o'er life's short span
 When forms we love decay:
Faith views the immortal inward man,
 And wipes the tear away.

And when we feel we cannot now
  Shelter one heart we prize
From many a conflict, many a woe,
  Or hush its secret sighs;

Then, as we see them onward borne,
  By time's resistless flow,
To that bright shore where none can mourn,
  Where glory crowns each brow;

Should we not hail their nearer bliss,
  When faith's sure hope is given!
What means "advancing age" but this,—
  The drawing near to heaven?

A Prayer at Midnight.

CELESTIAL SPIRIT! now, in this calm hour,
Thy meanest temple with Thy presence fill!
"I commune with my own heart, and am still,"
Waiting to feel Thy tranquillising power.
Darkness is around me; but, like that pale flower *

* The night-blowing Ceres.

Which loves its vestal fragrance to distil
When other flowers are closed, on dale and hill,
Breathed but for him who trained it for his bower,—
Thus, blessed Spirit! be it now with me;
In this poor heart, Thy consecrated shrine,
Thy hand has formed and trained a plant divine,
Unseen, unknown, unnurtured, but by Thee:
Now by the hidden perfume Thou hast given
Exhaled, like incense sweet, and borne to heaven!

The Wanderer's Return.

"Before I was afflicted I went astray."—*Ps.* cxix. 67.

LIGHT beams upon my inward eye,
  New thoughts awake, new things I see;
Is this "the day-spring from on high,"
    Shining on me?

The God of love my soul has met;
  He gently draws me from above;
And though I do not love Him yet,
    · I long to love.

My time of suffering and distress
   Has proved His time of pardoning grace;
Now, that He chastens but to bless
    I clearly trace.

Earth's vanities my soul beguiled,
   I never sought His will to know;
But to reclaim His wandering child,
    He brought me low.

The past appears a feverish dream
   Of folly, and insensate mirth,
And now the things eternal seem
    Of boundless worth.

My soul, once dead, begins to move,
   Roused by a Hand divine from sleep,
My heart, once cold, begins to love,
    My eye to weep.

Lord, while this heavenly light is shed,
   Which, while I gaze, seems still t' increase,
Shall not my wandering steps be led
    To paths of peace?

Light of the world! Thou, thou hast shone,
With life and healing in Thy ray!
Now clear my path, and lead me on
    To realms of day.

Go and Sin no More.

John viii. 11.

—◦—

SPEAK, my Saviour, speak to me,
With divine effectual power—
Weeping, I look up to Thee—
Bid *me* "go and sin no more."

Thou art full of pardoning love,
Thou canst grant what I implore;
Now Thy pitying mercy prove,
Bid me "go and sin no more."

Thou upbraidest not Thy child;
Deeply I the past deplore,
Now with gracious accents mild,
Bid me "go and sin no more."

Nothing can I see but sin,
It has tainted my heart's core;
There it spreads, without, within,
Can "*I* go and sin no more?"

'Tis for man too hard a task,
But Thou *canst* my soul restore;
Saviour! this alone I ask—
Bid me "go and sin no more."

Self-condemned—without a plea,
  Guilty—lost—like her of yore,
Mine may her acquittal be!
  Bid me "go and sin no more."

Oh, how blest will be that day
  When, while I Thy love adore,
I shall never need to say,
  Bid me "go and sin no more!"

On a Frosty Evening.

WHEN the dark mantle of o'ershadowing night
Wraps in concealment all the world below,
With countless orbs yon azure vault doth glow,
In silence shining, beautiful and bright,
The midnight wanderer gazes with delight,
And feels his heart within him overflow.
"O! what," he asks, "can day's broad sunshine show
To rival yon fair field of argent light?"
—'Tis sometimes thus when sorrow's mournful shade
Darkens our path, and veils our prospects here:

Fair worlds, unseen before, are then displayed,
And in surpassing majesty appear;
For then to faith's uplifted eye 'tis given
To view the glories of a brighter heaven.

The Hidden Life.

"Your life is hid with Christ in God."—*Col.* iii. 3.

OH ! there are some who, while on earth they dwell,
And seem to differ little from the throng,
Already to the heavenly choir belong,
And even here the same sweet anthem swell:
They joy, at times, with " joy unspeakable,"
Pouring to Him they love their heartfelt song;
While to behold Him " face to face" they long
As the parched traveller for the cooling well.
Ask you how such from others may be known ?
Mark those whose look is calm, their brow serene,
Gentle their words, love breathing in each tone,
Scattering rich blessings all around unseen.
They draw each hour, from living founts above,
The streams they pour around, of peace, and joy,
    and love.

Light and Darkness.

"The Lord God is a sun and shield."—*Psa.* lxxxiv. 11.

OH! if I walked by sight, not faith,
   And could not view the things unseen,
Dreary, to-day, would be my path,
   While round me wintry winds blow keen.

The driving sleet, the darkened air,
   Look bleak and mournful to behold,
While this poor frame, though fenced with care,
   Aches with the penetrating cold.

The glorious sun, whose gladdening beams
   Make e'en the face of winter smile,
Now distant and unwarming seems,
   Nature looks cheerless, for a while.

Heavenward I turn, and then on me
   Shines forth a warm, unclouded ray;
Sun of my soul! 'tis shed by Thee,
   I feel no more the wintry day.

Amidst th' external gloom Thy voice
   Speaks words of comfort to my heart;
Though weak, though lonely, I rejoice,
   Such gladness does that voice impart.

It tells me of those mansions blest
  Where Thou a place hast deigned prepare—
Where soon my soul shall sweetly rest—
  Where winter never chills the air.

It tells me of that blissful state
  Where there shall be no pain, no gloom,
Bids me a little moment wait,
  Till Thou shalt come to take me home.

My Saviour! through Thy love divine,
  Which all has pardoned, all bestowed,
I say, e'en now, "All things are mine,"—
  I possess all things in my God.

The Still Small Voice.

THERE is a Voice, "a still small Voice," of love,
              Heard from above;
But not amidst the din of earthly sounds,
              Which here confounds;
By those withdrawn apart it best is heard,
And peace, sweet peace, breathes in each gentle word.

The Still Small Voice.

In the sick chamber, oft when none are near,
   This Voice sounds clear ;
Then o'er the wearied frame, the suffering bed,
   Repose is shed :
Its whispers fall like balm upon the soul,
Each pang to soothe, each murmur to control.

Oft on the day of consecrated rest
   This unseen Guest
Visits the lonely and sequestered room,
   Dispels its gloom,
And pours such sacred melody around
That not an angel's harp more sweet could sound

In that appalling stillness which prevails
   Where nature fails,
When naught is heard save the convulsive breath,
   Struggling with death,
Then will this Voice of mercy gently break
That saddest silence, and of comfort speak.

Oh ! blessed then the sufferer, though he mourn,
   To whom are borne
The gracious accents of this heavenly Guide !
   None, none beside
Can calm the spirit, bend the opposing will,
And say, with Voice omnipotent, " Be still !"

To the Evening Star.

Lovely star! serenely shining
  On my heavy tearful eyes,
Thou shalt check these thoughts repining,
  And repress these mournful sighs;
    Let thy way be dark, or bright,
    Still thou shedd'st thy silvery light.

Still thy heavenly track pursuing,
  Rapidly thou hastenest on,
From that purer region viewing
  This dark world thou shin'st upon;
    Passing o'er it but to lend
    Light to gladden and befriend.

Thus, when clouds are passing o'er us,
  Grief our spirits may subdue;
But a race "is set before us,"
  And, though faint, we must pursue;
    Lovely star! our model be;
    May we shine through clouds like thee!

And, like thee, while freely lending
   Light to all within our sphere,
To our unseen centre tending,
   Swift as bright may we appear!
     Then, when thy brief course is o'er,
     We shall rise to set no more.

To a Widowed Friend.

WHY dost thou haste so swiftly on thy way,
Like one whose company before is gone?
What is that steadfast eye so fixed upon,
Beaming, at times, as with a heavenly ray?
Alas! that mourning veil, that dark array,
Tell me that thou from bitter grief hast won
A disentangled heart, no longer prone
To make terrestrial things thy staff and stay.
What though thy cheek be paler, lone thy path,
What though, unseen, sad memory tears will shed,
Now thou wilt live indeed the life of faith,
Till thou shalt meet again thy "holy dead."
Oh! if by grief such blessings here are given,
What "weight of glory" will be thine in heaven!

My Son, give Me thine Heart.

Prov. xxiii. 26.

———

FEELEST thou disquiet, care, unrest,
    Scarce knowing why so sad thou art?
In God alone can man find rest :
             Give Him thine heart.

Deem'st thou thy bosom's secret woes
    Peculiar, from all else apart?
Thy case He intimately knows :
             Give Him thine heart.

Oft doth the painful thought arise,
    That slighted, misconceived, thou art?
God knows thee, loves, will not despise :
             Give Him thine heart.

Sail'st thou alone o'er life's rough sea,
    Without a home, a friend, a chart?
Thy friend, guide, haven, God will be :
             Give Him thine heart.

Dost thou some hopeless sorrow feel,
    Some wound from Death's unpitying dart?
Thy God will bind it up, and heal :
             Give Him thine heart.

Are there some griefs thou canst not tell,
  Not to the dearest friends impart?
Thy God will understand them well:
      Give Him thine heart.

Oh! when without reserve 'tis given,
  Wholly surrendered, every part,
There shines within the dawn of heaven:
      Give Him thine heart.

The Christian near his Home.

I SEE an aged man
  Climbing the hill's steep side;
Long has he trod the pilgrim's way,
And now the sun's declining ray
  Homeward his steps will guide.
    A seat of rest
    Among the blest
E'en now awaits in heaven the dear expected guest.

His path is rough and steep,
More toilsome near its close :
The sky looks dark ; the winds blow keen :
The shadows lengthen o'er the scene,
And scarce a flowerlet blows :
 The pilgrim's eye,
 Still fixed on high,
Sees brighter worlds appear, beyond the darkening
 sky.

At times, indeed, he grieves
For earlier days more blest ;
When on the wings of joy he soared,
And, with an eagle's strength, explored
The land of promised rest ;
 But faith still shoots
 Its downward roots ;
The blossoms pass away, but riper grow the fruits.

Ill could he once have borne
His present toilsome path ;
He feels no joy, yet murmurs not,
This hushes each repining thought,.
 "While here, I walk by faith."
 He still can trace
 A Saviour's grace,   [face.
Though He appear far off, and seem to hide His

The heavenly prize he views,
And still maintains his ground;
The steep ascent is hard to win,
And many a foe, without, within,
Strives to inflict a wound;
Though closely pressed,
Hope cheers his breast;
For soon the strife will cease, the weary be at rest.

Pilgrim, the end is near!
Though faint, yet still pursue;
When thou shalt gain the mountain's brow
A scene beyond conception now
Shall burst upon thy view;
Celestial air
Shall fan thee there,
And thou shalt bid adieu to toil, and pain, and care.

Then thou shalt fall asleep,
And angels waiting round
Shall waft thee to that blissful shore,
Seen dimly from afar before,
Where golden harps resound;
Where souls set free
That Saviour see,
Whose smile is heaven itself:—that smile will beam
on thee.

Above the Heavens.

" As the heaven is high above the earth, so great is His mercy
toward them that fear Him."—*Psa.* ciii. 11.

I CAN gaze on that beautiful sky,
  Fair work of the Saviour I love ;
Though the health is withdrawn, and the vigour
      gone by,
  With which once 'mid His works I could rove.

I can gaze on that beautiful sky,
  And there in bright characters trace
That with mercy more great than that concave is high,
  My soul He has deigned to embrace.

I can gaze on that beautiful sky,
  That temple so worthy of Him ;
While the fabrics of earth seem to dwindle and die,
  Compared with its glory sublime.

I can gaze on that beautiful sky,
  And meekly rejoice in the thought,
That above it, in glory ne'er seen by the eye,
  A mansion for me He has bought.

I can gaze on that beautiful sky,
And long the blue pathway to tread;
There, with all His redeemed, to adore Him on high
For the blood He on Calvary shed.

I can gaze on that beautiful sky,
And rejoice that my Saviour from heaven,
In glory arrayed, will descend from on high,
While the clouds for His chariot are given.

Faint, yet Pursuing.

My body is weary and weak,
My spirits are low and depressed;
My Saviour! Thy sheltering wings I will seek,
For there is my refuge and rest.

Some message of love I shall hear,
Some whisper to comfort my heart;
Some gracious assurance to banish my fear,
Some promise new strength to impart.

The night of my life is far spent,
  Some streaks of the dawning I see;
Till the day-star arise and the vail shall be rent,
  My mind shall be stayed upon Thee.

One blessing alone I desire,
  The sense of Thy presence and love;
No more for my happiness, Lord, I require,
  Or here, or in mansions above.

The Skylark.

How sweet is the song of the lark as she springs
To welcome the morning with joy on her wings!
As higher she rises, more sweetly she sings,
  And she sings when *we* hear her no more.
When storms and dark clouds veil the sun from
    our sight,
She has mounted above them; she shines in his
    light;
There, far from the scenes that disturb and affright,
  She loves her gay music to pour.

It is thus with the Christian : he sees, from afar,
The Day-spring appearing, the bright Morning Star ;
He quits this dark valley of sorrow and care,
   For the land whence the radiance is given :
He sings on his way from this cloud-covered spot,
The swifter his progress, the sweeter his note :
When *we* hear it no longer, the song ceases not ;—
   It blends with the chorus of heaven.

Blessed are they that Mourn.

I HEARD the voice of Love divine,
   Addressing man, to trouble born ;
Saviour ! what accents then were Thine ?
      "Blessed are they that mourn."

Again it spoke—"Come unto Me
   "Thou, with distress and labour worn,
" Rest and refreshment are for thee :
      "Blessed are they that mourn."

172

I heard a voice in truth's pure word,
 A saint, who sorrow's yoke had borne,
"Blest is the man Thou chastenest, Lord!"
  "Blessed are they that mourn."

I heard an angel voice proclaim,
 Yon victors bright, whom crowns adorn,
"Through tribulation great they came!"
  "Blessed are they that mourn."

Why should I then for sufferings grieve,
 Since sorrow leads to joy's bright bourne?
Let me indeed the words believe,
  "Blessed are they that mourn!"

The Moon over the Sea.

Oh! FIX on that beautiful planet thine eye;
Observe her bright course as she travels on high,
And bears, like a vestal, her lamp through the sky,
 Arrayed in her garments of light:
While pure and exalted her pathway she treads,
O'er the rough sea beneath her, soft radiance she sheds;
Where'er she approaches, the darkness recedes,
 Till, in beauty, she glides from our sight.

Fair orb! there are some in this world of our own,
Like thyself, who in light and in silence move on;
They walk in "white raiment," and calmly look
 down
 On 'life's turbulent ocean beneath:
The noise of its waves at a distance they hear;
And, shedding soft light from their luminous sphere,
This region of darkness and sorrow they cheer,
 And are beautiful even in death.

For New Year's Day.

" What shall I render unto the Lord for all His benefits toward
me."—*Psa.* cxvi. 12.

I COME, my Lord, to offer up to Thee
 A worthless but a willing offering ;
A heart where only evil I can see,
 Yet not for that refuse the gift I bring;
Oh, deign to accept it—cast each evil out,
And make it pure and new within, without.

174

I come, my Lord, to offer up to Thee
  All it now suffers of distress and pain ;
It is Thine own ; work Thou Thy will in me ;
  Let me not once resist it, or complain,
But meekly in my sufferings acquiesce,
Assured that Thou each pang wilt deign to bless.

I come, my Lord, to offer up to Thee
  All that that heart can dictate or perform ;
Let Thy blest Spirit its controller be,
  Let Thy pure love its every movement warm ;
And make that heart, once sin's defiled abode,
The holy habitation of my God.

I come, my Lord, to offer up to Thee
  The brief remainder of life's fleeting span ;
Whate'er I have, or am, Thine own shall be,
  Without Thee I will form no wish nor plan :
Time, talents, influence, actions, thoughts, and words,
All, all be unreservedly my Lord's !

I come, my Lord, to offer up to Thee
  A creature made Thine own by every tie ;
Hast Thou not formed, preserved, and ransomed me ?
  Oh, didst Thou not to pay my ransom, die ?
Lord, at Thy feet my worthless self I lay,
Oh, never, never cast me thence away.

A Dream.

I WALKED upon an unknown shore;
   A deep, dark ocean rolled beside:
Thousands were wafted swiftly o'er
   That silent and mysterious tide.

Strange was the solemn scene, and new;
   My spirit sank with inward dread:
No voice proclaimed it; but I knew
   Those were the regions of the dead.

It was no earthly light that shone,
   Casting a shadowy gleam around;
Ne'er midst an earthly throng was known
   Stillness so awful, so profound.

The only sound which met the ear,—
   And sadly, heavily it fell,—
Was the dark billow rolling near,
   With measured, melancholy swell.

I sought with anxious eye to trace,
   Among the crowd that thronged the
The features of one well-known face,
   Fondly beloved, and lately lost.

The twilight gleam sufficed to show
  Full many a face that once was fair,
Now marked with characters of woe,
  The sad, sad impress of despair.

No words were needed to express
  Whose tears of anguish fell too late;
The dark fixed look of mute distress
  Declared too legibly their fate.

Some have been lovely once on earth,
  Caressed, applauded, loved, admired,
Endowed with riches, talents, birth,
  Possessing all their hearts desired.

Those hearts, alas for them! were given
  To earthly pleasures, cares, and toys;
They found not time to think of heaven,
  To seek imperishable joys.

Slowly I turned, with many a sigh,
  From this sad spectacle of woe;
And soon I saw the beaming eye
  Of her so fondly loved below.

She had but just been called away
  From husband, parents, children, friends;
Yet in that eye there shone a ray
  Of joy with which no sadness blends.

A Dream.

A bright companion at her side
  Looked on her with celestial love;
Delighting her glad steps to guide
  Towards the bright home prepared above.

Unseen I followed. It was sweet,
  Oh, passing sweet, her voice to hear:
No earthly language could repeat
  The sounds that then entranced my ear.

Swiftly we passed that gloomy shore;
  Darkness and clouds were all withdrawn:
And then a light, not known before,
  Began upon our path to dawn.

With growing strength I saw her tread
  Her upward, brightening, heavenward road,
With joy she lifted up her head,
  To hail the city of her God!

As nearer to that world we drew,
  Immortal fragrance filled the air;
But soon the increasing radiance grew
  Too bright for mortal sense to bear.

I only caught a distant glance
  Of glories, never to be told;
I saw a beauteous band advance;
  I heard them strike their harps of gold.

And then I lost her.—Faint and dead
　I sank beneath the eternal beam.
The sights, the sounds, the glories fled:
　"I woke,—and found it was a dream!"

To One Bereaved of many Relatives.

THOU hast laid up so many treasures there,
Where there is no more sorrow, no more pain,
That I esteem thee rich in heavenly gain,
E'en by the loss of those who dearest were.
Oh, while thy deepest, tenderest thoughts they share,
When sad and desolate thou sighest in vain
Their voice to hear, their smile to meet again,
Pour out thy heart, pour out thy griefs in prayer!
That blest employ will re-unite thy soul
With those whose adorations never cease:
That hallowed intercourse each grief control,
And o'er thy bosom shed celestial peace;
Though powerless human sympathy be found,
Sweet converse with thy God can heal each wound.

Anticipations.

————

WE gaily said, that when the Spring
Her opening buds and flowers should bring,
And happy birds begin to sing,
    We three would meet.

We planned full many a golden hour
Of bliss, within our favourite bower ;
And never thought a cloud would lower,
    That bliss to o'ershade.

While thus we framed our fairy schemes,
Adorned with Hope's enchanting beams,
And smiled at Fancy's lovely dreams,
    - And thought them true—

Death saw the visions Hope portrayed ;
The joys on Fancy's eye that played ;
And cast, o'er all the chilling shade
    Of his dark wing.

And now the scene, so bright before,
For us can never brighten more ;
Hope's fond illusions all are o'er,
    And Fancy's dreams.

And, if we meet in that loved bower,
No festive mirth will wing the hour;
For every plant and every flower
    Will wake our tears;

Will tell of her who loved to view
Each varied leaf, each beauteous hue;
Whose smile such sweet enchantment threw
    O'er all the scene.

When last we lingered, late and long,
Those moonlit woods and bowers among,
To woo the nightingale's sweet song,
    She shared our joy.

Little we thought that when again
That bird should pour its plaintive strain,
For *her* its melody in vain
    Would charm the sense.

Little we thought, when next the Spring
Sweet flowers and happy birds should bring,
Those flowers would bloom, those birds would
    Around her grave.   [sing,

But hush! ye sad repinings cease!
Her life was blest; her death was peace!
And now her joys will still increase
    Through endless years.

Epitaph.

Her's is a fairer world than ours;
She walks among unfading bowers;
And higher joys and nobler powers
    To her are given.

Indulge no more that rising sigh,
Turn not again thy tearful eye
To that sad spot where mouldering lie
    Her loved remains :

They do but slumber in the dust;
While angels guard their sacred trust
Till all the bodies of the just
    In glory rise.

Epitaph.

THE lamb is gathered into that blest fold
Where dangers cannot enter, nor alarms,
Led by her Shepherd, carried in His arms,
She passed through earth, scarce tarrying to behold
The " waters still," which near her gently rolled

On the "green pastures," decked with flowery
    charms;
But though we thought her sheltered from all harms,
This damp terrestrial climate proved too cold.
Her Shepherd watched her drooping, and meanwhile
" The everlasting arms " were underneath;
Cheered by His voice, encouraged by His smile,
She reached the dark unfathomed gulf of death,
He hushed its waves:—then to His fold above
Wafted safe o'er the object of His love.

On a Restless Night in Illness.

My Saviour! what bright beam is shed
Around my dark and suffering bed,
Though downy slumbers thence have fled?
       It is Thy peace.

When the sad fear of future ills
My trembling heart with sorrow fills,
What balm sweet quietude instils?
       It is Thy peace.

To One whose Mind was disordered.

When awful thoughts of death's dark hour
Like gathering clouds around me lower,
What to dispel them all has power?
      It is Thy peace.

When weary night and lonesome day
Cast mournful shadows o'er my way,
What then becomes my staff, my stay?
      It is Thy peace.

If suffering be my lot below,
Lord! till my tears shall cease to flow,
In life, in death, one boon bestow!
      It is Thy peace.

To One whose Mind was disordered by Grief.

MOURNER! thy spirit was too finely strung
For the rude climate of a world like this:
And while it breathed its notes of love and bliss,
On which the listener's ear delighted hung,
And deemed that such to heavenly harps are sung,
Too suddenly did that sweet music cease:—

Some angry blast the slender chords had wrung,
And changed its notes to murmurs of distress,
Mourner! that "harp of thousand strings" was
    framed
To breathe its music in a happier clime:
There shall its power melodious be reclaimed,
Though broken now, and tuneless, for a time:
Chords ever tuned, and ever strong be given,
And no rough wind the "new song" mar in heaven.

The Widowed Heart.

              Is thine a widowed heart?
             Each tie asunder torn;
       Does one sad wish alone remain,
       Swiftly to travel till thou gain
            The parted spirits' bourne?
             Wouldest *thou* fain sleep
             Where death doth keep
That slumbering form beloved, in delvèd chamber
         deep?

Poor, bleeding, widowed heart!
Man's words less heal than probe;
Not in man's pity canst thou find
Balm for thy wound, or power to bind;
Still must it bleed and throb!
Friends pitying mourn,
Then sadly turn
To hide their fruitless tears, and looks that o'er thee
yearn.

Alas! poor widowed heart,
What sorrows press on thee!
Each object that now meets thine eye,
Each hour that wearily goes by,
Remembrancers will be
Of joys all fled,
And smiles that shed   [dead.
Bliss o'er that rifled heart, where all but grief seems

Poor desolated heart!
If yet some joy remain,
If in thy lonely path so drear
One lingering uncrushed flower appear
To bid thee smile again,
Who now partakes
The smile it wakes,
Or culling it for thee, of tenfold value makes?

The Widowed Heart.

Alas! poor widowed heart!
No signs thy grief express;
No human eye beholds thy tears;
No ear thy sob of anguish hears;
In utter loneliness!
Calm, nay, serene,
Midst anguish keen,—
Thy deep, deep hidden wound by God alone is seen.

Alas! poor widowed heart!
The charms of infant glee,
Thy little ones' unconscious smiles,
Their prattled words and artless wiles,
Wake only grief in thee.
The eye they blessed,
The lip they pressed,
On them no longer beams, nor smiles, nor is caressed.

Alas! poor widowed heart!
What now will be thy stay?
The staff so fondly leant upon,
Thy guide, thy counsellor, is gone,
For ever torn away!
Each link unbound
Which clasped thee round,
No second self for thee, left all alone, is found!

For thee, poor widowed heart,
In vain sweet spring returns;
The charm of vernal songs and flowers,
The joys reviving nature showers,
Touch not the heart that mourns;
Or touch it so,
As wakes fresh woe
For one all darkly laid, this blooming earth below!

Yet, still, poor widowed heart,
Though desolate and sad,
The thought—thy mourned one ne'er can know
Thine own unutterable woe—
Almost might make thee glad!
The blest deplore
Earth's griefs no more;
And though thy joys are fled, thy loved one's tears
are o'er.

Poor broken, widowed heart,
To God disclose thy pain!
Earth yields no cure; but Heaven has given
A balm for hearts bereft and riven,
A balm ne'er tried in vain:
That volume bright,
Where beams of light
Illume the Eternal Words, reveals it to thy sight.

To a Bereaved Christian Friend.

MOURNER! is thy heart still grieving,
Secret tears sad traces leaving,
Frequent sighs thy bosom heaving?—
          Why dost thou weep?

Dost thou mourn those gone before thee?
Lost is not the love they bore thee:
They may now be watching o'er thee.—
          Why dost thou weep?

Though thy path on earth be shaded,
Has not death left uninvaded
Worlds of bliss and joys unfaded?—
          Why dost thou weep?

Hath not Christ thy sins remitted?
Will not thy glad soul, when fitted,
Into heaven be soon admitted?—
          Why dost thou weep?

Should the ills of life distress thee?
Grief, care, loneliness depress thee?
With thy Saviour near to bless thee,
          Why dost thou weep?

Ever near, to walk beside thee,
Near to counsel, guard, and guide thee ;
Say, can any ill betide thee ?—
   Why dost thou weep ?

Prayer to the Saviour.

O HOLY SAVIOUR ! Friend unseen !
The faint, the weak, on Thee may lean :
Help me, throughout life's varying scene,
  By faith to cling to Thee.

Blest with communion so divine,
Take what Thou wilt, shall I repine,
When as the branches to the vine
  My soul may cling to Thee?

Far from her home, fatigued, opprest,
Here she has found a place of rest ;
An exile still, yet not unblest,
  While she can cling to Thee.

Without a murmur I dismiss
My former dreams of earthly bliss;
My joy, my recompense be this,
    Each hour to cling to Thee.

What though the world deceitful prove,
And earthly friends and joys remove;
With patient uncomplaining love
    Still would I cling to Thee.

Oft when I seem to tread alone
Some barren waste with thorns o'ergrown,
A voice of love, in gentlest tone,
    Whispers, "Still cling to Me."

Though faith and hope awhile be tried,
I ask not, need not aught beside:
How safe, how calm, how satisfied,
    The souls that cling to Thee!

They fear not life's rough storms to brave,
Since Thou art near, and strong to save;
Nor shudder e'en at death's dark wave;
    Because they cling to Thee.

Blest is my lot, whate'er befall:
What can disturb me, who appal,
While, as my strength, my rock, my all,
    Saviour! I cling to Thee?

To Faith.

WRITTEN IN ILLNESS.

—•∞•—

COME, holy Faith! beside me stand,
　With look inspired, with eye serene!
Unfold the bright celestial land,
　　　　The world unseen!

Pleasant was once the earth's pure air;
　With rapture on its scenes I gazed:
Yet not to Him who made them fair
　　　　My heart was raised.

E'en by the beauty of His works
　That heart too oft was led astray:
Such danger unsuspected lurks
　　　　In Pleasure's way.

But now those charms no more delight;
　Earth's beauteous face is hid from me:
Still, holy Faith, in thy pure light
　　　　Much I may see!

I shall not sigh to breathe the gale
　Perfumed with buds and flowers of spring,
If thy pure ray heaven's scenes unveil,
　　　　And near me bring.

A brighter sun will cheer my sky,
  And make e'en this dark chamber sweet,
Than e'er in crimson canopy
        Has risen or set.

And sounds more blest than song of bird,
  Or rills and whispering boughs impart,
Shall in this silent room be heard,
        And cheer my heart.

Why should I Fear to Die?

I NEED not fear to die,
  My Lord has conquered death;
And He has promised to draw nigh
  When I resign my breath.
His word is truth—on that I build,
Assured that word shall be fulfilled.

Sometimes I long to die!
  My nest is stirred up here;
Earth's ties are few; I long to fly
  To a serener sphere:
Where sin, and toil, and war shall cease;
And all be holiness and peace.

Why should I Fear to Die?

Why *should* I fear to die?
  In that sweet home above
Are gathering all my family,
  And all the friends I love;
Heavenward I look, and breathe the prayer,
Soon, soon their happiness to share.

Surely 'tis time to die!
  My "threescore years and ten"
Are overpast, and oft I cry,
  "How long, my Lord? Oh! when
Wilt Thou my ransomed spirit free,
And bid Thy child come home to Thee?"

Then, Saviour, *let* me die!
  My sweetest moments here
Are those when, deigning to draw nigh,
  Thou whisperest, "I am near."
And e'en from these bright glimpses given
I feel Thy presence must be heaven.

Oh! when I come to die,
  These glories let me see,
Ne'er grasped by human thought or eye,
  Reserved in heaven by Thee;
And show me, 'mid the parting strife,
That death is better far than life!

Thy Will be Done.

My God and Father, while I stray
Far from my home in life's rough way,
Oh, teach me from my heart to say,
   "Thy will be done!"

Though dark my path and sad my lot,
Let me "be still" and murmur not;
Or breathe the prayer divinely taught,
   "Thy will be done!"

What though in lonely grief I sigh
For friends beloved, no longer nigh,
Submissive still would I reply,
   "Thy will be done!"

Though Thou hast called me to resign
What most I prized, it ne'er was mine:
I have but yielded what was Thine :—
   "Thy will be done!"

Should grief or sickness waste away
My life in premature decay;
My Father! still I strive to say,
   "Thy will be done!"

Let but my fainting heart be blest
With Thy sweet Spirit for its guest;
My God! to Thee I leave the rest:
    "Thy will be done!"

Renew my will from day to day!
Blend it with Thine; and take away
All that now makes it hard to say,
    "Thy will be done!"

Now we see through a Glass, darkly.

1 Cor. xiii. 12.

As through a glass, half clear, yet half concealed,
I view those glories soon to be revealed;
But who can comprehend, till he shall die,
What "life and immortality" imply?
A life without a want, without a tear,
Freed from our inward conflict and its fear;
Where none shall witness, none experience pain;
I strive to realise such life in vain.
And then that awful hour (on earth the last),
That strange, mysterious transit will be passed;

196

Will o'er the future cast its shade no more;
What will it be to feel that death is o'er?
Thou ! who hast oped once more those golden gates,
Closed by the sin of Adam, there awaits
The bright-winged form of *Immortality*—
There let her bid *me* welcome, when I die.

On Leaving Home.

THIS gracious promise, Lord, fulfil,
　　Now that I leave a home so dear:
My soul's sweet home is present still
　　　　If Thou art near.

Beneath Thy wings if I remain,
　　My home ! my hiding-place ! my rest !
Sheltered, and safe, and freed from pain,
　　　　My soul is blest.

Thy presence fills my mind with peace,
　　Brightens the thoughts so dark erewhile,
Bids cares and sad forebodings cease,
　　　　Makes all things smile.

This striking of my pilgrim tent
　No longer mournful will appear,
If Thy reviving presence lent
　　The traveller cheer.

The spacious earth is all thine own;
　What land soe'er my steps invite,
That land Thine eye will rest upon
　　By day, by night.

I ask not health—I ask not ease,
　I ask in Thee my rest to find;
To all *Thy* sovereign will decrees,
　　Be *mine* resigned!

Guide every step where'er I go;
　Dictate each action, word, and thought;
With those "fresh springs" from Thee that flow,
　　Let all be fraught!

If soon my sun of life shall set,
　Still let me work, ere sinks that sun:
Nor mourn at last with vain regret
　　My task undone.

Link me with those who fear Thy name,
　Whose zeal, and faith, and love shine bright,
And let them feed my lamp's weak flame
　　With their pure light.

Whether again my home I see,
  Or yield, on foreign shores, my breath,
Take not Thy presence, Lord, from me,
      In life or death!

In Thee, my hiding-place divine,
  Be rest throughout life's journeyings given,
Then sweeter, holier rest be mine
      With Thee in heaven!

Be not Faithless, but Believing.

O FAINT and feeble-hearted!
  Why thus cast down with fear?
Fresh aid shall be imparted;
  Thy God unseen is near.
His eye can never slumber:
  He marks thy cruel foes,
Observes their strength, their number;
  And all thy weakness knows.

Though heavy clouds of sorrow
  Make dark thy path to-day,
There may shine forth to-morrow
  Once more a cheering ray.
Doubts, griefs, and foes assailing,
  Conceal heaven's fair abode ;
Yet now, faith's power prevailing,
  Should stay thy mind on God.

Leaning on her Beloved.

WRITTEN FOR ONE NOT LIKELY TO RECOVER.

LEANING on Thee, my Guide, my Friend,
  My gracious Saviour ! I am blest ;
Though weary, Thou dost condescend
    To be my rest.

Leaning on Thee, this darkened room
  Is cheered by a celestial ray :
Thy pitying smile dispels the gloom—
    Turns night to day.

Leaning on Thee, my soul retires
From earthly thoughts and earthly things;
On Thee concentrates her desires;
    To Thee she clings.

Leaning on Thee, with childlike faith,
To Thee the future I confide;
Each step of life's untrodden path
    Thy love will guide.

Leaning on Thee, I breathe no moan,
Though faint with languor, parched with heat:
Thy will has now become my own—
    Thy will is sweet.

Leaning on Thee, midst torturing pain,
With patience Thou my soul dost fill:
Thou whisperest, "What did I sustain?"
    Then I am still.

Leaning on Thee, I do not dread
The havoc slow disease may make;
Thou, who for me Thy blood hast shed,
    Wilt ne'er forsake.

Leaning on Thee, though faint and weak,
Too weak another voice to hear,
Thy heavenly accents comfort speak,
    "Be of good cheer!"

Leaning on Thee, no fear alarms;
  Calmly I stand on death's dark brink:
I feel "the everlasting arms,"
    I cannot sink.

Return unto thy rest, O my Soul.

Oh! when the exile views his home;
  The banished child his father's face;
The traveller, long condemned to roam,
  His native fields, his resting-place;

What sweet emotions fill the mind!
  What joy, what blessedness they feel!
My God! these joys are all combined
  When at Thy mercy-seat I kneel.

Thou art my dwelling-place, my rest,
  My Father, in whose smile I live:
All I desire to make me blest,
  That smile alone can amply give.

No longer now my thoughts I waste
   On earthly things once loved by me :
For sweeter, purer joys I taste,
   My God, in communing with Thee.

Safe on the other Side!

"The fear of death is fallen upon me."—*Psa.* lv. 4.

OH, let my faith these tears control,
Still, still I dread the unfathomed tide !
What will it be to find my soul
     Safe on the other side !

What will it be to hear that voice
Which bids each trembling fear subside?
In His sweet presence to rejoice
     Safe on the other side !

To see His beauty, taste His love,
Be with His likeness satisfied ;
To know I ne'er can thence remove,
     Safe on the other side !

To feel that all my bonds are riven,
This weary body cast aside,
To know that I. am safe in heaven!
    Safe on the other side!

No death to fear, no cross to bear,
No more to hear His truth denied
To know sin cannot enter there:
    Safe on the other side!

To meet our loved ones "gone before!"
To see them blest and glorified!
To know that we can part no more,
    Safe on the other side!

All this, and joys so vast, so great,
As human thought ne'er verified,
Are laid up in that glorious state,
    Safe on the other side!

And yet with coward fears I shrink
From passing through that gulf untried—
Oh! haste thee quickly, cross the brink,
    Safe to the other side!

Jesus! Thou conqueror of death!
My hope, my shield, my guard, my guide,
Waft me, Thy sheltering arms beneath,
    Safe to the other side!

Thoughts on a Birthday.

Day before which I was not! day ordained
  Life mortal and immortal to bestow!
First, that in which the soul for heaven is trained,
  Then, that of glory, which no end shall know.
Day of my birth! I welcome thee, and pray
Each year may lend new brightness to thy ray.

Day of deep thoughts and feelings! when the past
  Borne on the tide of memory rises dark,
And many a plank, and shivered sail, and mast
  Tell of the storms that wellnigh wrecked my bark;
Day of regrets and sorrows! welcome still!
There's medicine in the bitter they distil.

Day of high hopes and arduous resolves,
  And kindling thoughts, which grasp things un-
    attained,
When the fixed mind its history revolves—
  All it has learned, felt, suffered, lost and gained;
And asks that deep within each lesson taught
May there, by Thee, indelibly be wrought.

Day of bright retrospection! when the soul
  Swells high with gratitude for mercies showered,
Counts o'er the record, twelve brief months unroll,
  But sinks beneath the summary, overpowered ;
Day of adoring thankfulness and praise,
To higher strains of love my spirit raise.

Oh be thou to me, each revolving year,
  A monitor more welcome and more dear ;
A heaven-sent messenger, glad news to bring,
  And added swiftness to my spirit's wing ;
Pouring within, around a purer ray,
" Brighter and brighter to the perfect day."

By the Death-bed of a Friend.

" He giveth His beloved sleep."—*Psa.* cxxvii. 2.

LIE down in peace to take thy rest,
  Dear cherished form, no longer mine,
But bearing in thy clay-cold breast
  A hidden germ of life divine,
Which, when the eternal spring shall bloom,
Will burst the shackles of the tomb.

By the Death-bed of a Friend.

Lie down in peace to take thy rest,
  Unbroken will thy slumbers be,
Satan can now no more molest,
  And death has done his worst on thee ;
Lie down, thy hallowed sleep to take,
Till clothed with glory thou shalt wake.

Lie down in peace to take thy rest,
  We can no longer watch thy bed ;
But glorious angels, spirits blest,
  Shall guard thee day and night instead ;
And when thine eyes unclosed shall be,
Christ in His glory they shall see.

Lie down in peace to take thy rest !
  My eyes must weep—my heart must mourn ;
But to the thought that thou art blest,
  For comfort and for hope I turn ;
Thou wilt not mark these tears that flow,
Sorrow can never reach thee now !

Lie down in peace to take thy rest !
  Let *me* betake myself to prayer,
Binding faith's corslet on my breast,
  Lest Satan find an entrance there ;
God gave—though now His gift He claim,
Still blessed be His holy name !

Hymn for a Dying Bed.

WHILE ceaseless love and ceaseless care
 By all are fondly shown,
A voice within me cries, "Beware!
 For thou must die *alone*."

That solemn hour is come for me,
 Though all their charms I own,
When human ties resigned must be;
 For I must die alone.

Terrestrial converse now is o'er;
 My work on earth is done;
And I must tread th' eternal shore,
 And I must die alone.

But oh! I view not now with dread
 That shadowy vale unknown;
I see a light within it shed:
 I shall not die alone!

One will be with me there, whose voice
 I long have loved and known:
To die is now my wish, my choice,
 I shall not die *alone!*

Prayer for a Departing Spirit.

FATHER! when Thy child is dying,
On the bed of anguish lying,
Then, my every want supplying,
      To me Thy love display!

Let me willingly surrender
Life to Thee, its gracious lender:
Can I find a friend more tender?
      Why should I wish to stay?

Ere my pulse has ceased its beating,
Ere my sun has reached its setting,
Let me, some blest truth repeating,
      Shed round one parting ray.

Ere my chain's last link be broken,
Grant some bright and cheering token,
That for me the words are spoken—
      "Thy sins are washed away!"

If the powers of hell surround me,
Let the accuser not confound me;
All for which Thy law once bound me,
      Thyself hast died to pay.

P

Prayer for a Departing Spirit.

When no remedies availing,
Fiercer pangs my frame assailing,
Show that flesh and heart are failing,
  Be Thou my strength and stay!

When, though tender friends are near me,
Their kind pity cannot cheer me,
And they strive in vain to hear me,
  Turn not Thy face away!

When, each face beloved concealing,
Death's dark shade o'er all is stealing,
Then, Thy radiant smile revealing,
  Unfold eternal day!

When the lips are dumb which blest me,
And withdrawn the hand that pressed me,
Then, let sweeter sounds arrest me,
  Calling my soul away.

When, in silent awe suspended,
Those who long my couch have tended,
Weeping, wish that all were ended,
  Oh, hear them when they pray!

When my soul, no path discovering,
O'er my lifeless form is hovering,
Then with wings of mercy covering,
  Be Thou Thyself my way!

Safe in Christ.

" My sheep hear My voice, and they shall never perish; neither shall any pluck them out of My hand."—*John* x. 27, 28.

CLOUDS and darkness round about Thee
 For a season veil Thy face,
Still I trust—and cannot doubt Thee,
 Jesus ! full of truth and grace :
Resting on Thy words I stand,
None shall pluck me from Thy hand.

Oh, rebuke me not in anger !
 Suffer not my faith to fail !
Let not pain, temptation, languor,
 O'er my struggling heart prevail !
Holding fast Thy word I stand,
None shall pluck me from Thy hand.

In my heart Thy words I cherish,
 Though unseen, Thou still art near;
Since Thy sheep shall never perish,
 What have I to do with fear ?
Trusting in Thy word I stand,
None shall pluck me from Thy hand.

The Perfect Example.

"Let this mind be in you, which was also in Christ Jesus."—*Phil.* ii. 5

EVER patient, gentle, meek,
   Holy Saviour! was Thy mind;
Vainly in myself I seek
   Likeness to my Lord to find;
Yet that mind which was in Thee,
May be, must be formed in me.

Days of toil, 'mid throngs of men,
   Vexed not, ruffled not thy soul;
Still collected, calm, serene,
   Thou each feeling couldst control:
Lord, that mind which was in Thee
May be, must be formed in me.

Though such griefs were Thine to bear,
   For each sufferer Thou couldst feel;
Every mourner's burden share,
   Every wounded spirit heal;
Saviour! let Thy grace in me
Form that mind which was in Thee.

When my pain is most intense,
  Let Thy cross my lesson prove :
Let me hear Thee, e'en from thence,
  Breathing words of peace and love :
. Saviour ! let Thy grace in me
Form that mind which was in Thee.

Not my Will, but Thine.

"Let them that suffer according to the will of God commit the
keeping of their souls to Him."—1 *Peter* iv. 19.

O GOD ! from whom my spirit came,
Moulded by Thee, this mortal frame
Feels health or sickness, pain or ease,
As it may best Thy wisdom please :
Make me submissive—keep me still,
Suffering according to Thy will.

The springs of life are in Thy hand,
They move, they stop at Thy command ;
Without Thy blessing will prove vain
All human skill to ease my pain :
Make me submissive—keep me still,
Suffering according to Thy will.

I am a sinner—shall I dare
To murmur at the strokes I bear?
Strokes, not in wrath, but mercy sent,
A wise and needful chastisement:
Make me submissive—keep me still,
Suffering according to Thy will.

Saviour! I breathe the prayer once Thine,
"Father! Thy will be done, not mine!"
One only blessing would I claim;
In me O glorify Thy name!
Make me submissive—keep me still,
Suffering according to Thy will.

Thou God seest Me.

"When my spirit was overwhelmed within me, then Thou knewest
my path."—*Psa.* cxlii. 3.

My God! whose gracious pity I may claim,
Calling Thee "Father," sweet endearing name!
The sufferings of this weak and weary frame,
All, all are known to Thee.

From human eyes 'tis better to conceal
Much that I suffer, much I hourly feel;
But oh, this thought can tranquillise and heal,
    All, all is known to Thee.

Each secret conflict with indwelling sin;
Each sickening fear, "I ne'er the prize shall win;"
Each pang from irritation, turmoil, din,
    All, all are known to Thee.

When in the morning unrefreshed I wake,
Or in the night but little rest can take,
This brief appeal submissively I make,
    All, all is known to Thee.

Nay, all by Thee is ordered, chosen, planned,
Each drop that fills my daily cup, Thy hand
Prescribes for ills none else can understand,
    All, all is known to Thee.

The effectual means to cure what I deplore,
In me Thy longed-for likeness to restore,
Self to dethrone, never to govern more,
    All, all are known to Thee.

And this continued feebleness—this state,
Which seems t' unnerve and incapacitate,
Will work the cure my hopes and prayers await,
    That cure I leave to Thee.

Nor will the bitter draught distasteful prove,
While I recall the Son of Thy dear love;
The cup Thou wouldst not for *our* sakes remove—
    That cup He drank for me.

He drank it to the dregs—no drop remained
Of wrath—for those whose cup of woe He drained:
Man ne'er can know what that sad cup contained:
    All, all is known to Thee.

And welcome, precious, can His Spirit make
My little drop of suffering for His sake;
Father! the cup I drink—the path I take,
    All, all are known to Thee!

A Present Help.

"God is our refuge and strength, a very present help in trouble."
Psa. xlvi. 1.

GOD of pity! God of love!
Send me comfort from above;
Let not anxious thoughts perplex,
Harrowing fears my spirit vex:
Let me trust Thee, and be still,
Waiting patiently Thy will.

Though to weak short-sighted man
All uncertain seems each plan;
Each event Thy will ordains,
Fixed immutably remains:
Not one link in life's long chain
Can be lost, or wrought in vain.

All that chain, through bygone years,
Woven in links of love appears;
Not one storm of vengeful wrath
E'er has swept across my path:
Why should fear o'er faith prevail?
Thy sure mercies cannot fail.

What are distance, time, or place,
To that God who fills all space?
What are sea or land to Him?
Can the Omniscient eye grow dim?
Those we love, (whate'er betide,)
O'er them does that eye preside.

Clinging to Thy strengthening arm,
Thou wilt keep me safe from harm;
Thou wilt grant the hope that cheers
Will prove better than my fears;
Bid my sad misgivings cease;
Guide me to my home in peace.

Paternal Chastening.

" If ye endure chastening, God dealeth with you as with sons."
Heb. xii. 7.

Oh cheer thee, cheer thee, suffering saint !
Though worn with chastening, be not faint !
And though thy night of pain seem long,
Cling to thy Lord—in Him be strong,
He marks, He numbers every tear,
Not one faint sigh escapes His ear.

Oh cheer thee, cheer thee ! He has traced
Thy track through life, from first to last ;
Each stage, the present, childhood, youth,
Has borne fresh witness to that truth :
Which soon will tune thy harp above,
" Loved with an everlasting love."

Yes, cheer thee, cheer thee ! though thine ear,
Quickened by suffering, scarce can bear
The voice of those who love thee best,
Not lonely art thou, not unblest ;
Thy soul's Beloved ever nigh
Bends o'er thee, whispering, *" It is I !"*

Oh cheer thee, cheer thee! now's the hour
To Him to lift thine eye for power,
His all-sufficiency to show,
E'en in extremity of woe:
While in the furnace to lie still,
This is indeed to do His will.

Then cheer thee, cheer thee! though the flame
Consume thy wasting, suffering frame;
His gold ne'er suffers harm or loss,
He will but purge away the dross,
And fit it, graced with many a gem,
To form His glorious diadem.

And He will cheer thee, He will calm
Thy pain intense with heavenly balm,
Show thee the martyr's white-robed throng,
Thy place prepared that host among;
That weight of glory will o'erpower
The anguish of life's suffering hour.

Yes, He *will* cheer thee—He will prove
The soul encircled by His love
Can meekly, midst her anguish, say,—
"Still will I trust Him though He slay;"
And He will make His words thine own—
"Father! Thy will, not mine, be done."

Strong Consolation.

" I will not leave you comfortless."—*John* xiv 18.

Holy Comforter! who guidest
   Those who seek Thine aid divine!
Who in contrite hearts abidest,
   Now, amidst my darkness, shine!
Though around me waves are swelling,
   And the storms of life increase,
If my heart be made Thy dwelling,
   I shall still be kept in peace.

'Tis Thine office, blessed Spirit!
   Christ's remembrancer to be;
Though such grace I cannot merit,
   Now recall His words to me;
Though with grief my heart seems broken,
   Though the waves go o'er my soul;
Every word, by Jesus spoken,
   Makes the wounded spirit whole.

God of peace and consolation!
   Pour this balm upon my mind;
In my Saviour's Cross and Passion
   Strength and healing let me find!

Is the outward man decaying?
  Be the inward man renewed!
Now, Thy power and love displaying,
  Cheer my mournful solitude.

Take the things to Christ belonging,
  Manifest His love to me;
Check these thoughts of anguish, thronging
  This poor heart, resigned to Thee;
Show me life nor death can sever
  From my soul that heavenly Friend,—
Tell me He is mine for ever,
  And will love me to the end.

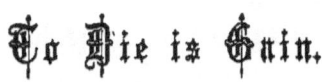

To Die is Gain.

Phil. i. 21.

O MUCH beloved! fear not to die,
Lift up to heaven thy tearful eye;
  And see, prepared for thee,
A mansion where no sins, no foes,
Shall ever break thy sweet repose,
  Through all eternity.

221

Why should'st thou fear to die, when death
Is but to yield thy mortal breath,
   And lay this frame aside,
"Fearfully, wonderfully made"—
Yet now, enfeebled, worn, decayed,
   And oft with suffering tried?

Death *must* dissolve it; flesh and blood
Can enter not that pure abode
   Where Christ His face unveils:
Then since by death, and death alone,
Can be attained that bliss unknown,
   Shrink not when death assails.

To Nature his approach seems sad,
But Faith rejoices, and is glad
   His coming step to hear:
She knows that though the hand be rough
That strikes the soul's hard fetters off,
   Each blow brings freedom near.

Then when the captive is set free,
What life, what joy, what liberty
   Will heaven's bright gates unfold!
The last pang felt, the last sigh heaved,
Faith's great reward will be received,
   Christ Jesus to behold!

Christ in His glory! oh, the thought
With bliss ineffable is fraught;
   And when the soul holds fast
That blessed hope which He has given,
Of endless life with Him in heaven,
   Aside all fears are cast.

Then, much beloved, fear not to die!
Lift up by faith thy tearful eye,
   And see, in heaven prepared,
A place where near Him thou shalt be;
Where by thyself, eternally,
   His glory shall be shared.

Prayer against Impatience.

Lord, when I see Thee as Thou art,
   No sufferings then will wake a sigh;
Grant the one wish that fills my heart,
   To glorify Thee ere I die!

When I would murmur and complain,
   Fix on Thy cross my tearful eye;
Mine is far lighter to sustain;
   Oh, make me patient ere I die!

What countless blessings Thou hast given,
  Though health it please Thee to deny,
Thy precious blood—a home in heaven!
  Oh, make me thankful, ere I die!

Thou art my stem, my life, my root:
  Sap to Thy feeblest branch supply;
Those who "abide in Thee" bear fruit—
  Oh, make me fruitful, ere I die!

Too often do I go astray;
  Unstable—weak—alas! am I;
Oh, keep me in Thyself, my Way;
  Make me consistent, ere I die!

Oh, prove, by making all things new,
  Thou dost within me rule, not I;
Let grace the carnal mind subdue,
  And make me heavenly, ere I die!

None without holiness can see
  Thy glorious beauty, "eye to eye:"
But if my heart Thy temple be,
  I shall be holy, ere I die.

Let every grace combine to prove
  Thy Spirit seals me from on high;
Faith, meekness, resignation, love,
  Let each adorn me, ere I die.

Show that I am in Thee "complete;"
 In me Thy mercy magnify;
Let all around Thy praise repeat,
 By me awakened, ere I die.

Thou art the Lord my Righteousness,
 No other wedding robe need I;
Jehovah's eye no spot will trace,
 In it arrayed I'm fit to die.

This, this alone can safety give
 When death's appalling hour draws nigh;
If it be "Christ" to me "to live,"
 It will be "gain" indeed "to die."

The Unfailing Friend.

" He hath said, I will never leave thee nor forsake thee."—*Heb.* xiii. 5.

THE thought that I must leave, ere long,
 My friends beloved, at times will grieve me;
But this, e'en then, shall be my song,—
 The Lord will never, never leave me.

Well mayest Thou ask, O Friend Divine,
  "Am I thy God? dost thou believe Me?"
Lord, 'tis enough if Thou art mine,
  If Thou wilt never, never leave me!

Whither I go my friends will come,
  Death will enrich and not bereave me;
Will waft me to that blessed home
  Where Thou wilt never, never leave me.

From the rough passage shall I start
  When there Thou waitest to receive me?
When I shall see Thee as Thou art,
  And Thou wilt never, never leave me.

Thou'rt gone my mansion to prepare,
  Thou art the Truth—canst Thou deceive me?
Soon Thou wilt reunite us there,
  Nor e'er forsake nor ever leave me!

For a Sunday in Solitude.

LET me put on my fair attire,
  My heavenly "robes of richest dress,"
And tune my consecrated lyre,
  Lord of the Sabbath! Thee to bless.

For a Sunday in Solitude.

Oh, may no spot of sin to-day
　My raiment, " clean and white," defile !
And while I tune my heartfelt lay,
　Bend down on me Thy gracious smile.

Let holy feelings, heavenly themes,
　Raise and refresh and fill my mind !
And earth's low vanities and schemes
　Nor place nor entertainment find !

The looks, the thoughts, the sweet employ
　Of saints, whose treasure is above,
Be mine to-day—their zeal, their joy,
　Their peace, and purity, and love.

My spirit may with theirs unite,
　My humble notes with theirs may blend,
Though still denied the pure delight
　Thy sacred courts with them t' attend.

" The faith and patience of the saints,"
　These I may exercise each hour ;
When, weak with pain, the body faints,
　I best may manifest their power.

Oh, Saviour ! with completion crown
　Desires Thou wakenest not in vain ;
Stoop to Thy lowly temple down :
　Bring all these graces in Thy train.

I come to Thee.

This is Thy day of bounty, Lord!
  I ask no small, no stinted boon,
But showers, rich showers of blessing, poured
  On me, though worthless and alone.

If the weak tendril round *Thee* twine,
  It ne'er is hidden from Thine eye;
I cling to Thee, life-giving Vine!
  Strength, verdure, fruitfulness, supply.

I come to Thee.

" Into Thine hand I commit my spirit: Thou hast redeemed me,
O Lord God of truth."—*Psa.* xxxi. 5.

GOD of my life! Thy boundless grace
  Chose, pardoned, and adopted me;
My rest, my home, my dwelling-place!
    Father! I come to Thee.

Jesus, my hope, my rock, my shield!
  Whose precious blood was shed for me,
Into Thy hands my soul I yield;
    Saviour! I come to Thee.

Spirit of glory and of God !
    Long hast Thou deigned my guide to be ;
Now be Thy comfort sweet bestowed !
    My God ! I come to Thee.

I come to join that countless host
    Who praise Thy name unceasingly ;
Blest Father, Son, and Holy Ghost !
    My God ! I come to Thee.

Forsake Me Not.

" Be not Thou far from me, O Lord ; O my strength, haste Thee
to help me."—*Psa.* xxii. 19.

FORSAKE me not, my God, my heart is sinking,
    Bowed down with faithless fears and bodings vain ;
Busied with dark imaginings, and drinking
    Th' anticipated cup of grief and pain ;
But, Lord, I lean on Thee ; Thy staff and rod
      Shall guide my lot,
I will not fear if Thou, my God, my God,
      Forsake me not !

Forsake me not, my God! man must forsake me,
    And earth grow dim, and vanish from my sight;
Through death's dark vale no human hand may take
    me,
    No friend's fond smile may bless me with its light :
Alone the silent pathway must be trod
        Through that drear spot,
For I must die alone—Oh then, my God,
        Forsake me not.

Forsake me not, my God! when darkly o'er me
    Roll thoughts of guilt, and overwhelm my heart;
When the accuser, threatening, stands before me,
    And trembling conscience writhes beneath the dart;
Thou who canst cleanse, by Thine atoning blood,
        Each sinful spot,
Plead Thou my cause, my Saviour and my God !
        Forsake me not.

Forsake me not, O Thou, Thyself forsaken,
    In that mysterious hour of agony,
When, from Thy soul, Thy Father's smile was taken,
    Which had from everlasting dwelt on Thee !
Oh, by that depth of anguish which to know
        Passes man's thought,
By that last bitter cry, incarnate God,
        Forsake me not !

In Sleeplessness or Pain.

CELESTIAL GUARDIAN ! Thou who slumberest not,
Does not Thy gracious eye behold the spot
On which this weak and weary frame reclines,
Though now no cheering light around me shines?

Oh yes ! with heavenly pity Thou look'st down
On me, e'en me, whose sins deserve Thy frown ;
Gild now th' oppressive darkness with Thy smile,
And these sad hours of restlessness beguile.

Though sweet repose forsake my uneasy bed,
Like silent dew Thy grace benignant shed ;
If Thou beside me these night-watches keep,
Thy presence will refresh far more than sleep.

The restless, feverish body Thou canst calm,
And on th' unquiet mind drop healing balm ;
Canst round the soul such cheering radiance pour,
That outward darkness shall be felt no more.

Oh Thou ! who, when on earth, would'st oft repair
To some lone mount, and pass the night in prayer,
Set free my spirit from its cumbrous clod,
And be these waking hours all spent with God.

In Deep Waters.

" Forasmuch then as Christ hath suffered for us in the flesh, arm yourselves therefore with the same mind."—1 *Peter* iv. 1.

WHEN passing through deep waters
   Of bitter pain and grief,
That sun is veiled which scatters
   The clouds of unbelief;
When past sins gather round me
   In all their crimson hue,
And foes unseen confound me
   With taunts, alas! too true—

When human hopes all wither,
   And friends no aid supply;
Then whither, Lord, ah, whither
   Can turn my straining eye?
'Mid storms of grief still rougher,
   'Midst darker, deadlier shade,
That cross, where Thou didst suffer,
   On Calvary was displayed.

On that my gaze I fasten,
   My refuge that I make;
Though sorely Thou mayest chasten,
   Thou never canst forsake:

Thou on that cross didst languish
  Ere glory crowned Thy head ;
And I, through death and anguish,
  Must be to glory led.

***

On Recovery from Illness.

"Not my will, but Thine, be done."—Luke xxii. 42.

IT is Thy will; my Lord! my God!
And I, whose feet so lately trod
  The margin of the tomb,
Must now retrace my weary way,
And in this land of exile stay,
  Far from my heavenly home.

It is Thy will; and this, to me,
A check to every thought shall be,
  Which else might dare rebel ;
Those sacred words contain a balm
Each sad regret to soothe and calm,
  Each murmuring thought to quell.

It is Thy will; that will be done!
To Thee the fittest time is known,
   When, by Thy grace made meet,
My longing soul shall soar away,
And leave her prison-house of clay,
   To worship at Thy feet.

It is Thy will; and must be mine,
Though here, far off from Thee, I pine,
   And find no place of rest;
When shall the poor bewildered dove,
Now, o'er the waters doomed to rove,
   Be sheltered in Thy breast?

It is Thy will; and now anew
Let me my earthly path pursue
   With one determined aim;
To Thee to consecrate each power,
To Thee to dedicate each hour,
   And glorify Thy name.

It is Thy will; I seek no more;
Yet, if I cast towards that bright shore
   A longing, tearful eye,
It is because, when landed there,
Sin will no more my heart ensnare
   Nor Satan e'er draw nigh.

More than Conqueror.

"We are more than conquerors through Him who hath loved us."
Rom. viii. 37.

HARK! what voice of love is speaking
　'Mid these throes of pain and death?
Light upon my soul is breaking
　E'en while struggling thus for breath;
Welcome, then, this dying anguish,
　These cold dews that steep my brow!
That blest hour for which I languish
　Cannot be far distant now!

All my outward senses, failing,
　Part me from terrestrial things;
But my soul, new life inhaling,
　Fluttering, striving, spreads her wings;
Ye, who tenderest watch are keeping—
　Though these hours seem dark indeed—
Think, while o'er my sufferings weeping,
　Thus th' imprisoned soul is freed.

Be the prison bars demolished!
　King of terrors, break them down!
But, thy further power abolished,
　Christ thy conqueror thou must own:

235

He is with me, He is near me!
He thy every stroke directs!
His belovèd accents cheer me,
He the soul He saved protects!

Lord, Thou comest to receive me!
Oh, what faithfulness is Thine!
Now, when every friend must leave me,
Come to be for ever mine!
Lo! the beatific vision
Breaks on my enraptured sight!
Weighed with this divine fruition
E'en the pangs of death seem light.

When Expecting Suffering.

"Call upon Me in the day of trouble, I will deliver thee, and thou
shalt glorify Me."—*Psa.* l. 15.

My GOD! the dreaded hour draws near,
Nature shrinks back, and faints with fear,
My heart within me dies;
But still on Thee, who know'st my frame,
Who torture hast endured, and shame,
On Thee my hope relies.

When Expecting Suffering.

I make no arm of flesh my stay—
All human powers Thy will obey—
  All means on Thee depend—
Whate'er that will appoint for me,
In life, in death, Thine let me be,
  Support me to the end!

Give me that faith which nerves the soul,
That love which can all fear control,
  Which "all things can endure;"
Now, in my time of utmost need,
My Saviour! let me find indeed
  Thy word of promise sure.

Stand by me—speak those words divine,
"I have redeemed thee, thou art Mine,
  "Thee will I ne'er forsake;"
Say to my agitated heart,
Nothing from Thee my soul shall part,
  Nor Thy sure covenant break.

And if a creature so defiled,
Whom yet Thou deign'st to call Thy child,
  May ask one boon beside,
'Tis this—that in my suffering hour
Thy grace may manifest its power,
  Thy name be glorified.

Abba, Father.

" Ye have received the spirit of adoption, whereby we cry,
Abba, Father."—*Rom.* viii. 15.

THOU, who searchest every heart,
   Bend on mine Thy pitying eye!
Pardon, cleansing, peace, impart,
   Abba, Father, hear my cry!

Grant that pardon Christ implored
   From His cross on Calvary;
Through my dying, pleading Lord,
   Abba, Father, hear my cry!

Water from His side, and blood,
   Flowed to wash sin's deepest dye;
Bathe me in that cleansing flood,
   Abba, Father, hear my cry!

Earthly cares and woes increase,
   But from them to Thee I fly,
Jesu's legacy was peace—
   Abba, Father, hear my cry!

238

Dark may be life's mournful day,
    Still no tear should dim my eye ;
This sweet name drives grief away,
    Abba, Father, hear my cry !

Pardon, cleansing, peace, impart,
    All my need through Christ supply ;
With His Spirit fill my heart,
    Abba, Father, hear my cry !

The Sheltering Wing.

My Saviour ! when I come to die,
Look down on me with pitying eye,
    For Thy sweet mercy's sake ;
Shield my foreboding, trembling heart,
From the accuser's fiery dart !
    Thy wings my covering make !

Thou knowest, Lord, my only plea
Is sovereign grace, too rich, too free,
    Too omnipotent to doubt ;
It drew me—led me to Thy feet ;
To hear Thee those 'blest words repeat,
    " Ne'er will I cast thee out."

239

In childhood, through that grace divine,
To Thee my heart did I resign;
   And though in after years
I wandered far in sin's dark track,
Mercy pursued and brought me back,
   With floods of contrite tears.

Still has that mercy led me on;
For more than "forty years" has shone
   O'er life's long pathway traced;
And now, methinks, I see it gleam
From far, o'er Jordan's billowy stream,
   Whither my footsteps haste.

Saviour! Thy voice can banish fear,
And if Thou deignest to draw near
   When most I need Thine aid;
If, when the cold waves round me swell,
"The everlasting arms" I feel,
   I shall not be dismayed!

Mercy will bear me safely through,
Mercy, sweet mercy, still pursue,
   Brightening the dark rough wave,
And land me on that peaceful shore
Where enemies are known no more,
   Omnipotent to save.

All Things become New.

O HEAVENLY traveller! hasting
From scenes where nought is lasting,
Its glimmering lamps all wasting,
    Earth darkens on thy view;

While now, the world forsaking
The pilgrim's path thou'rt taking,
What light around thee breaking
    Makes every object new!

When earthly joys have faded,
And when, by grief invaded,
Those spots are all o'ershaded,
    Once bright in life's fair morn;

Then, beams from heaven descending,
With each dark shadow blending,
A lovelier radiance lending,
    The Christian's path adorn.

Nor fear to lose their shining,
Like earth's poor stars declining;
No! more, yet more refining,
    This light will bless thy way.

R

O'er hill and valley streaming,
O'er death's dark river beaming,
The dawn progressive seeming
    Of heaven's eternal day.

The Ever-present Helper.

"Lord, be thou my helper."—*Psa.* xxx. 10.

WHEN all outward comfort flies,
And my heart within me dies,
Hear, oh hear my trembling sighs:
    Help me, O my Saviour!

When the day brings pain and grief,
Night, nor respite, nor relief,
Whisper—"These dark hours are brief:"
    Help me, O my Saviour!

When all human help proves vain,
And my agonising pain
More than nature can sustain.
    Help me, O my Saviour!

242

Suffer not my faith to fail,
Let not Satan's darts assail,
Lift the intercepting vail :
    Help me, O my Saviour !

When, oppressed with feverish heat,
I can scarce one text repeat,
Say, I am in Thee complete :
    Help me, O my Saviour !

When the means for pain's redress
Seem to aggravate distress,
Then draw near—my faith increase :
    Help me, O my Saviour !

When the long and suffering night
Makes me weary for the light,
Fix upon Thy cross my sight :
    Help me, O my Saviour !

Lest I faint beneath the rod,
Say—"This very path *I* trod;
"Thus *thou* glorifiest God :"
    Help me, O my Saviour !

Let me not on man depend,
But on Thee, the unfailing Friend :
Be Thou near me to the end :
    Help me, O my Saviour !

Closing Sonnet.

Thou, Thou only canst relieve me!
Till Thine arms of love receive me,
Whisper—" I will never leave thee!"
Help me, O my Saviour!

Closing Sonnet.

THOU! who all seasons rulest, and canst bless
Dark sorrow's Winter and joy's Summer bright,
Whose smile preserves our life's sweet flowers from
    blight,
And gives its richest bloom to happiness,—
That smile sheds radiance even o'er distress:
And if it beam, these winter flowers to dress
In hues refreshing to the aching sight
Of those whom this world's flowers no more delight,
The gatherer's heart will glow with thankfulness.
I place them on Thy shrine, to bloom or fade
As it may please Thee,—worthless at the best,
Still by this offering love may be expressed,
Which thinks on griefs it vainly longs to aid.
O, should they cheer one sufferer,—one alone,
Thine be the glory! all the praise Thine own!

APPENDIX.

—•◦•—

NOTE A.

AMONGST the innumerable testimonies to the value of the hymn "*Just as I am*," the following, from the son-in-law of the poet Wordsworth, will be read with interest:

LOUGHRIGG HOLME, AMBLESIDE:
July 28, 1849.

DEAR MISS ELLIOTT,

The day I received your very kind and welcome note, with the music of the hymn, I was moving from home, and I did not return till last night. I need not say how much I am obliged to you. That hymn was originally sent to us, for my dying wife, by a relation of ours, a clergyman's wife in Kent; and it is rather remarkable that *her* daughter, who is on a visit to us, was the first person (as yet the only one) from whom I heard the music, which is exactly what it should be. This young lady was in the room when I received it, and she immediately, at my request, sang it without difficulty to her own accompaniment. I should be ashamed of having deprived you of your only copy; but you tell me that you have access to another. I cannot desire more touching and appropriate melody for the words; but, if you will not think me obtrusive and unreasonable, I *should* like to have the other air, when your niece may have leisure to copy it; for everything connected with those words cannot but be of the deepest interest to me, and to Mr. and Mrs. Wordsworth.

When I first got the letter enclosing them, from Kent, I said to the beloved sufferer who knew she was soon to leave us, "Here is a hymn from your friend Charlotte —— of Barham. Shall I read it to you?" She answered hesitatingly, "Yes, I *must* hear it since it comes from *her*. She is so good, it ought to be worth hearing." I read it; and had no sooner finished than she said very earnestly, "That is the very thing for me." At least ten times that day she asked me to repeat it to her; she desired me to write it in "Horne's Manuel for the Afflicted," a little book which she kept by her pillow, and which is now one of my melancholy treasures; and, every morning, from tbat day till her decease nearly two months later, the first thing she asked me for was her hymn. "Now *my* hymn," she would say—and she would often repeat it after me, line for line, many times in the day and night. You may judge from this whether the volume you propose to send us will be acceptable to her father and mother and husband.

Mrs. Wordsworth has told me that your hymn forms part of her daily solitary prayers. I do not think that Mr. Wordsworth could bear to have it repeated aloud in his presence, but he is not the less sensible of tbe solace it gave his one and matchless daughter.

The place you date your note from, Torquay, disturbs me with a fear; but I hope the delicacy of your health is in no way connected with the malady that has made me desolate for the rest of my term.

Believe me, dear Miss Elliott, with true sympathy,

Your obliged and faithful friend,

EDWARD QUILLINAN

Appendix.

THE following is the original of the letter from Dr. Cæsar Malan, of which a translation is given on page 17.

MANCHESTER: 18 *Mai*, 1822.

BIEN CHÈRES AMIES,

Puisque le Seigneur, notre Dieu, notre Sauveur et Père, a daigné me faire "trouver grâce auprès de vous," et que la parole de son ministre vous a été agréable et précieuse, je puis, en paix et avec confiance, continuer à vous entretenir de ces choses qui "appartiennent à nôtre éternel salut."

L'amour du Seigneur est au-dessus de toutes ses œuvres ; ses compassions sont plus élevées que les cieux, et il n'oublie aucune des ses promesses ; il est fidèle. Nous ne le croyons pas, chères amies ; notre cœur ne peut ni supposer, ni admettre l'*amour* que Dieu a pour nous, à moins que la puissante grâce de Dieu ne l'ait changé, renouvelé, retourné vers le Seigneur. Même parmi le monde chrétien : au milieu de ceux qui parlent le plus abondamment de religion, ce qui se trouve le moins, ce qui s'y fait le plus rarement apercevoir, c'est le sentiment simple et sincère de l'amour de Dieu. On peut s'entretenir durant des heures sur l'évangile, sur les *affaires* des Églises : on peut savamment et spirituellement discourir sur quelque haute doctrine, quelque point de morale ; on peut ainsi faire dire et se persuader à soi-même "qu'il y a eu beaucoup d'édification dans telle visite, telle réunion, telle assemblée, et néanmoins demeurer aussi loin de la vie de Dieu, que les gens du monde le sont dans leurs calculs ou leurs vaines poursuites."

Bonnes amies, un seul regard silencieux mais arrêté et fidèle sur la croix de Jésus vaut mieux que tout cela, et il a plus de puissance. Il est du moins en rapport avec l'éternité : c'est un regard de vie, oui, de vie divine. Se dire qu'on est aimé de l'Éternel ; qu'il *est notre* Père ; qu'il nous *chérit*, qu'il nous voit, nous suit, nous guide, et nous garde ; *croire*, mais croire, en effet, que Jésus est notre ami, de tous les jours, de toutes les heures, que sa grâce nous entoure, que sa voix nous invite continuellement à être saint et heureux en lui ; demeurer, comme un enfant, dans la joie de cet amour et répéter à son âme : "O mon âme, mon âme, demeure en repos et bénis ton Dieu ;" tout cela qui est la vie ; et sans quoi il n'y a point de vie ici bas et dans le monde supérieur, tout cela n'est pas l'œuvre de notre volonté ; c'est l'immédiat accomplissement de la puissance miséricordieuse et toute gratuite de Celui qui est éternellement heureux, "qui est amour, et qui veut être appelé et reconnu, le Père de toute compassion."

Mais, chères, oui vraiment chères amies et sœurs, nous pouvons dans notre vanité, dans une folle présomption ; dans un égarement ridicule, nous pouvons nous flatter de vivre en dehors de cette vie : d'être sage loin de cette vérité ; d'être contents, heureux, paisibles, au milieu de notre propre agitation, et dans un sentier que nous *voulons* tracer parmi le sable mouvant de notre gloire, de l'approbation de nos alentours, de nos sciences, de nos lectures, de nos plaisirs, etc., etc. Alors, et bien-heureusement, O ! Charlotte ! alors il n'y a plus de paix pour une âme immortelle ainsi abusée, liée, et dix fois vaincue par la ruse et la séduction de Satan, du monde, et de sa propre folie. Il n'y a pour cette âme là qu'une secrète inquiétude, une longue langueur ; des larmes, des regrets, et des continuels soupirs vers une vie qu'elle ne peut saisir, et dont elle sent l'impérieux besoin.

Mais, mais, Jésus demeure le même au-dessus de cette

ténébreuse ignorance ; de ce coupable égarement ; Jésus, dont le nom est Sauveur ; Jésus qui n'épie point une pauvre âme pour la trouver en faute, et la perdre ; mais pour l'attirer à lui, et lui rendre la vie en lui pardonnant tout. Jésus regarde cette âme, et cette chère âme, s'étonne d'être de nouveau sensible ; de trouver des larmes de repentance, des espoirs de grâce, et de pardon ; des joies qu'elle avait cru ne plus connaître—Jésus regarde Pierre, et Pierre peut ensuite lui dire " *Tu sais* que je t'aime." Eh bien ! mes bien chères amies, puisque un tel regard est parvenu sur vos chères âmes, puisqu' aujourd'hui vous pouvez dire " *Nous avons trouvé le Messie* "—et vous réjouir dans le regard de sa face, demeurez-vous dans cette glorieuse possession, en demeurant *simples*, Oui, *simples* et en ne vous occupant, durant ces premiers temps surtout, que de cette bénédiction, que de cette joie ; O ! laissez, je vous en prie au nom de votre Rédempteur, de votre Roi, qui veut régner sur TOUT votre cœur, laissez donc les occupations de Marthe, et soyez heureuses d'être tranquilles au pied du Sauveur écoutant ce que LUI a à vous dire.

Chère Héléna, offrez-vous à Christ en *sacrifice*, en holocauste ; ne lui retranchez rien de votre cœur. Chère Charlotte, coupez les cables ; il serait trop long de les délier ; coupez-les ; c'est une petite perte ; le vent souffle et l'océan est devant vous,—l'Esprit de Dieu, et l'Éternité.

Votre Frère et Ami,

C. MALAN.

Que vos chers parents se rapellent de moi dans leurs prières !

NOTE C.

There is a touching history associated with the hitherto unpublished Hymn inserted on **page 52** of the Memoir, commencing:

> " Darling, weep not! I must leave thee,
> For a season we must part !"

A copy of it, written out for the purpose by Mrs. Babington, was, in the month of November, 1872, forwarded by a friend to Lord Shaftesbury, then at Mentone, suffering under a double affliction—the recent loss of a deeply-beloved wife, and the threatened removal of his second daughter, on whom the tenderest affection of both her parents had been centred during several years of failing health. The hymn was given to Lady Constance Ashley by her sorrowing father, and was found after her joyful death, on the 16th of December, fastened to the fly leaf of a Bible which had been his gift. Her remains were brought to England, and the following account, which mentions Miss Charlotte Elliott's hymn, appeared in the *Record* of December 30, 1872:

> " The funeral of Lady Constance Ashley was solemnized on Friday last in the church of St. Giles's, Wimborne, with

much simplicity. Great was the sympathy felt with her noble father and the rest of his family; for, like Lord Shaftesbury's other daughters, she had endeared herself to the parishioners, when in health, by visiting the cottages and almshouses, and attending both to their temporal and spiritual wants. Her departure at Mentone was the beautiful close of a short but beautiful life. A holy resignation tempered her deep grief for the death of a mother, the tenderness of whose maternal devotion to her invalid daughter during years of suffering could not be surpassed. Her own departure more resembled a translation than a death scene. Shortly before the end, she called her surviving parent to her bedside, blessed him for all he had done for her, and fondly charged him not to give way to sorrow, but to continue his noble career in his Master's service. To her sorrowing sisters she spoke with the same tenderness, and to her younger sister she repeated from an unpublished poem of the late Charlotte Elliott (the writer of the almost heaven-inspired hymn ' Just as I am '), three stanzas beginning :

> " Sweet has been our earthly union,
> Sweet our fellowship of love;
> But more exquisite communion
> Waits us in our home above."

She then said, ' Christ is very near me.' ' I am waiting to hear Him say, "Come, blessed of my Father."' When reminded by Lord Shaftesbury of her blessed mother's favourite expression, ' Simply to Thy cross I cling,' all heaven seemed to shine out in her face radiant with joy, and she unmistakeably intimated her cordial assent. Her last words were addressed to her pious nurse, "I know I am going to die, for I feel so happy." She then turned her head on her pillow, fell into a sweet sleep, and expired soon afterwards without a struggle or a sigh."

On a wall of the church of St. Giles, Wimborne, a marble tablet has been affixed, near one which contains a glowing tribute of affection to the memory of the Countess of Shaftesbury, with the following inscription :

TO THE MEMORY OF

CONSTANCE EMILY,

A deeply-beloved daughter, whose suffering life and joyful end were a rich example of the truth of her chosen text :

" For me to live is Christ,
And to die is gain."—*Philip*. i. 21.

SHAFTESBURY.

At Mentone, Dec. 16, 1872, God took her unto Himself.

INDEX OF FIRST LINES.

Index of First Lines.

Index of First Lines.

THE END.

www.ingramcontent.com/pod-product-compliance
Lightning Source LLC
Chambersburg PA
CBHW031406020726
47499CB00005B/1485